To Amy.

This is th[illegible] ...tion
of "Perkins Per[illegible]s"
Take good care of it and
always eat your vegetables!

Perkins Perfect Parents

D Fisher

Diane Banham

Perkins Perfect Parents

Cover design by Leanne Brown at Sirenic Creations

dianebanhamimagine@outlook.com

No cats, ducks or socks were harmed in the creation of this book.

Unfortunately I cannot say the same for the chocolate cupcake!

For T and his marvellous mind.

Chapter 1

The Weasel Faced Man

Ladies and gentlemen, may I present

'THE BOREDOM SWITCH'

Possibly the best invention ever to come from Tom's 10 year old brain. This nifty little gadget beats boredom with just one simple flip of a switch. Fully portable it can be carried discreetly in any size pocket ready for use at the appropriate time. Tedious family get togethers, wearisome weddings, colourless christenings, unexciting parent's evenings and even humdrum homework can be obliterated with one flick.

This invention was going to make Tom a millionaire, no a zillionaire or even better the world's first gazillionaire. Every child around the globe would want one, Tom had used his so many times now he'd lost count.

There was just one problem…. it didn't exist!

Bored stiff, bored to death, bored to tears however he said it there was no shaking the fact at this precise moment Tom was mind-numbingly finger flicking BORED.

How is it even possible to be this bored he silently screamed inside his head and with a huge shoulder sinking sigh sank deeper into his chair.

Tom was as bored as a bored person bored with being bored! I think you get the idea.

He had quickly decided hospitals were not his favourite place, they smelt weird and were full of grown-ups fussing over wrinkly new babies that cried and smelt of mouldy milk.

Fidgety, hot and utterly fed up he sat swinging his feet impatiently on his sticky plastic coated chair until they could leave, which seemed like forever.

The grown-ups didn't seem to understand he had far more important places to be like exploring with his friends, no he had to sit here and be a good new big brother.

B-O-R-I-N-G!!!!

"Aw, look Tom he's smiling at you," gushed Gran as the pink wrinkly bundle in her arms stared at him and grinned followed by a dribble of white milky vomit that ran from the corner of his mouth.

"Yes Gran," Tom mumbled in a not listening kind of way, he was too distracted watching that suspicious man across the ward.

Tall, lean and weasel faced he gracefully glided between the adults greeting each one with a smarmy smile. A flat cap kept his grey slicked back hair covered and a crisp white shirt under a heavy grey suit displayed a perfectly knotted blue tie. The whole ensemble was topped off with a long tan raincoat that flapped as he moved.

He must be boiling, why on earth does he need a raincoat? thought Tom. He was sweltering in the hospital heat wearing only his shorts and T-shirt but oddly the suspicious man looked as cool as a cucumber.

Tom's head hurt as it burst with questions. He certainly wasn't a doctor, or a nurse and he didn't seem to be with any particular group of parents, so what was he doing? Why was no one questioning why he was there and what was on the blue papers he was discreetly handing out to everyone? One thing was for sure Tom did not trust him one little bit.

"Come on young man, let's go and see if we can find you a cold drink and maybe a cheeky bar of chocolate," said Grandad with a boredom sensing wink. Steering

Tom with a protective hand on his shoulder they left the bustle of the baby ward behind and escaped to the welcome quiet of the corridor.

"Phew peace, at last. Your Gran will be in there for hours if she has her way," said Grandad turning his whistling hearing aid back up.

Apparently, he had to turn it down when spending long periods with Gran so he could hear her better. Tom knew otherwise.

"It will take a braver person than me to tackle trying to get her to leave when visiting hours are over. Now young man I think the vending machines are this way."

Tom grabbed his chance, “Grandad did you see that man?” as their footsteps echoed in the quiet uncluttered space.

“No Tom what man was that?” Grandad asked strangely avoiding eye contact and looking a little anxious at the question.

“The man in the ward, with the raincoat and cap whispering to everyone, you must have seen him he stood out like a sore thumb?”

“Nope sorry lad, I didn’t. Lots of people come and go in these places maybe he was a visitor or one of the staff?”

“No, he seemed odd something was….”

"Ah-ha, here we are," announced Grandad loudly cutting Tom's questioning off as the machines came into view. "Now what would you like anything you want my treat, and I may just join you in a chocolate bar, but don't you dare tell your gran."

Tom sighed, that was the end of that conversation he knew the signs. Making his chocolate choice Tom pressed the buttons and the machine whirred into life. Grandad meanwhile headed to the coffee machine and started chatting to a tired looking man nursing a large cup of steaming black coffee.

"Yes this is our first and it's home time for us today. I don't think we will be getting much sleep for a while," said the man not knowing whether to groan or smile as he turned to walk away.

"Well, all the best and it does get easier. Believe me, sleep does return eventually," promised Grandad stirring his froth topped drink and reaching for a naughty sugar or two.

Collecting their treats from the machine Tom sauntered towards his grandad when he saw something out the corner of his eye. A piece of blue crumpled paper drifted from the tired man's pocket. This was Toms chance, like a flash he snatched it from the floor stuffing it into his pocket before anyone noticed.

"Ah, there you are. Have you got everything?"

Tom nodded as he pushed a chunk of chocolate the size of a small car into his mouth and handed over the secret 'don't tell Gran' chocolate bar.

Grandad had the most amazing ability of hiding chocolate or in fact, anything unhealthy from Gran. It was like a magic trick he had mastered over their many years of marriage. She never caught him, not once which was a track record Grandad was extremely proud of. He had managed to finish the whole bar and dispose of any evidence before they strolled casually back into the ward.

"I wish I knew how you did that Grandad."

"Tricks of the trade my boy," winked Grandad sucking the final tiny smidgeon of chocolate from his thumb and patting him on the shoulder. "You'll learn one day."

The weasel faced man, to Tom's dismay, had vanished and as the bell rang to signal the end of visiting hours Tom hugged his exhausted mum. Nonchalantly licking her thumb she rubbed away a chocolate smear from the corner of his mouth before planting a kiss on his head. Everyone said their goodbyes, even a reluctant Gran, and taking Dads hand

Tom followed his grandparents from the ward.

"Come on lad we can all squeeze into the lift if we breathe in," said Grandad patting his belly in jest as they walked towards the shiny metal doors and pressed the button.

"No Grandad, we'll race you to the bottom," challenged Tom excitedly as he pulled his dad towards the stairs. Turning to watch the lift doors close Tom's mouth dropped in horror, there standing behind his grandparents was the man. The strange weasel faced man was in the lift, where had he materialised from?

"Grandad look the…," started Tom pointing but Dad grabbed his hand and rushed him down the stairs as fast as they could go. “Dad wait,” puffed Tom, “the man, the man in the lift did you see him?”

“No son, what man? I only saw Gran and Grandad, you must be seeing things. Knowing your grandad you’ve had far too much sugar, you’re not the only one that knows his crafty tricks.”

Fearing for his grandparent’s safety Tom hurtled down the stairs ready to confront the man no one else seemed to see.

Bursting through the ground floor doors Dad yelled triumphantly, “Come on Tom I think we’ve won,” at the precise moment the lift appeared.

Ping! the doors glided opened and out stepped Gran and Grandad chattering away without a care in the world. Tom stared into the empty lift with a look of disbelief on his face.

"But he was right there, the man where did he go?"

"Oh come on silly pants, let's go home and get everything ready for mum and baby Williams homecoming tomorrow," insisted Gran as she ushered him swiftly towards the exit.

There it was, that glance, the one from the eye corners grown-ups gave each other when they all knew something but weren't telling him. Tom knew it, every kid knows that look but what did it mean?

Honestly, grown-ups can be so annoying (I should know dear reader I am one).

Reaching into his pocket Tom checked the precious crumpled blue paper was safely hidden before clambering into the car. That would tell him what was happening he was sure, all he had to do was wait until they got home.

Chapter 2

Sneaky Strategies

Slamming the car door Tom rushed to the house waiting impatiently for Dad to find his keys.

“Hey, hey young man don’t push what’s the hurry?” asked Dad as Tom barged past them all and up the stairs.

"Erm, I need the toilet I'm busting," he called back darting into the bathroom, "and I wouldn't come in for a while it may not be safe," he added as the door closed behind him.

"Just make sure you flush it this time Tom I don't want any more of your surprises."

"Got it Dad."

Finally alone Tom pulled the blue paper from his pocket and smoothed it out on the cold tiled floor. A shimmer of gold lettering reflected on his face as Tom read something that was about to change his life forever.

Perkins School for Perfect Parents

proudly presents your

PERSONAL INVITATION

Dedicated to the fine art of crafty control and sneaky strategies we at Perkins pride ourselves in turning even the newest parents into perfect parents.
Learn the techniques and tricks of the trade proven to give results through countless generations.

Beginners, advanced or professional courses available.

SO JOIN US TODAY AND TEACH YOUR LITTLE ANGELS THE PERKINS WAY.

"NO WAY," Tom yelled louder than planned before slapping his hand across his gaping mouth.

"Is everything alright in there dear?" asked Gran softly tapping on the bathroom door.

"Erm yes Gran sorry, don't come in here it may take a while to flush this one it's a doozy," replied Tom grabbing the loo handle and hastily flushing it.

"Well make sure you put the lid down and wash your hands when you've finished," said Gran just like she did *every* time Tom went to the bathroom. "and don't use too much…."

"…paper, no I won't Gran," finished Tom as she walked away.

Several fake flushes later and a quick run of the tap to pretend he'd washed his hands Tom checked the hallway was grown-up clear. Rushing to his bedroom he closed the door quietly behind him and launched himself under his bed.

Rummaging in the odd socks and indescribable things that lurked in the shadows he finally pulled out his faithful walkie talkie. Yes, they were old school and of course everyone had phones, but walkie talkies were non-data chewing and more importantly untraceable by snooping parents who paid the bill.

"Ben, Sid are you there?… over."

Silence...

"GUYS PICK UP RIGHT NOW IT'S AN EMERGENCY…over."

"Alright keep your hair on nutter I'm here. Where have you been, you've been gone ages?" came the reply as Ben's familiar voice crackled down the speaker.

"Please tell me you have not been sat in that horrible hospital all this time. How did your brain not melt from boredom?" chipped in Sid.

"Never mind that no time to explain but you guys are not going to believe this. Get your bikes and meet me outside pronto."

"What? why?" stuttered Ben confused.

"Copy that big T," crackled back Sid.

"Dad I'm going out with Ben and Sid, and yes I will be back at 5 on the dot for tea. Love you," yelled Tom predicting the usual instructions as he ran through the wine drinkers in the kitchen and out of the back door.

Ben, Sid and Tom had been best friends since the first day of nursery school. They were the Three Amigos, The Three Musketeers or as their mums jokingly called them The Terrible Trio. They shared everything, went everywhere together and had a best mates bond that would never be broken (or at least until they became teenagers and discovered girls).

Ben, who lived across the street, was waiting with his bike by Toms front gate as instructed.

"What's going on why the hurry?" he yelled as Tom zipped past him hurtling towards Sid who was pedalling full pelt down the street.

"Come on I'll fill you in when we get to Pippin."

Across the streets, through the park and past the creepy old church the three boys raced until they reached the familiar gnarly apple tree in Farmer Welbury's field (otherwise known as Sid's Grandpa). Abandoning their bikes in a twisted heap they clambered into the scrub and bushes pushing open a concealed door.

This was their safe place, no one else was aloud and certainly not girls or grown-ups they were the den rules. Old pallets and spare wood had been dragged from the farm and nailed haphazardly together, then covered with plastic sheets and old animal feed bags to make it watertight.

The walls and floor had been lined with Sid's nan's old flowery carpet and the roof camouflaged with bundled branches and dried bracken. Half an old faded stable door Sid's grandpa had given them finished it all off. It wasn't elegant but it was theirs and many a plot had been hatched here, Den Pippin rocked.

"What does it mean crafty control and sneaky strategies?" asked Sid frowning at the scrunched blue paper as Tom filled them in.

"No idea," pondered Ben, "but anything that involves parents being crafty and sneaky doesn't sound good. That's a kid's job, not a grown-ups."

"Well that man was certainly crafty and super sneaky, he gave me the creeps," shuddered Tom as goose bumps crawled up his arms. "I still don't understand where he disappeared to, or how my gran and grandad didn't see him in the lift. He was standing right behind them, practically touching them."

"Hold on," piped up Sid as a thought sparked in his usually distant mind. "You said he was giving these papers to everyone in the ward, so maybe your mum and dad got one."

Tom thought for a moment, "I don't think so, no I'm sure they didn't. Why would they need one their just Mum and Dad they don't need teaching how to be a parent they've been doing it for the last 10 years with me. If they learnt from anyone it was Gran and Grandad, not some silly school."

"I've never heard of a school around here called Perkins, have you?" questioned Ben. Being the school football team captain meant Ben had played at all of them so he would remember the name.

"Maybe it's something at the college my sister goes to," suggested Sid. "They teach all sorts about childcare and all that horrible icky little kid's stuff."

"It could be, but it says Perkins *School*, so you'd think it would be a real building, but where?"

"Well one thing is for sure, our parents don't go," said Sid in relief. "We'd know if they did, they spend all day at work or in the coffee shop by the park nattering. They sure don't have time to go to some crafty parents school as well."

"Hey, don't moan about the coffee shop. Dad brings me a treat from there every Monday and Friday when he gets home from work," said Ben.

"Yeah, me too and when our mums meet on a Tuesday, we get something as well remember?" reminded Tom.

A yell came across the field, "SIDNEY WELBURY ARE YOU IN THAT DEN?"

All eyes shot towards Sid.

"YES GRANDPA."

"WELL, YOU HAD BETTER GET A WRIGGLE ON, YOUR MUMS ON THE PHONE. SHE SAYS YOUR PIZZAS GOING COLD AND IF YOU'RE NOT BACK BY 5 THEN YOU ARE GROUNDED AND YOUR GAMES CONTROLLER IS GONE FOR THE WEEK."

"Oh what is it with the games controller and parents?" exclaimed Ben throwing his arms in the air.

'I don't know but mine will be gone as well if I'm not home for tea, and Dad will have great pleasure in waggling his finger at me whilst he lectures me for the umpteenth time about responsibility," sighed Tom grabbing the mysterious blue paper and stuffing back into his pocket.

"ON MY WAY GRANDPA," shouted Sid as all three scrambled from the den. Untangling their bikes they peddled across the cowpat covered field and headed for home against the ticking clock.

"He's on the way Peggy, yes love I used the games controller line and threw in the grounded card just for safe measure. Yes, you're right it probably is the best thing they ever taught us," Grandpa chuckled as he hung up the phone.

5:02 and out of breath Tom burst in through the back door.

"Here, I'm here," he announced with a red face as his heart pounded like a caged animal trying to break free from his chest.

Gran was in the process of dishing up her famous steaming Shepard's Pie. It's delicious gravy and baked cheese smell filled the kitchen whilst Grandad set the table.

Looking at Tom over his glasses he sucked the air in through his teeth and whistled “Now that’s what I call cutting it fine.”

“Wash your hand’s young man and hurry back to the table, you could grow potatoes under those fingernails,” instructed Gran. “Oh, and you had better tell your dad you are home as he has just this minute gone to find your games controller.”

“DAD I’M HOME,” hollered Tom as he hurried into the downstairs cloakroom squeezing past the coat rack that bulged intrusively into the hallway. Hastily washing his hands he scrubbed the last of the dirt off with the now not so white hand towel and exploded from the cloakroom door.

"Woah slow down," cried Dad catching Tom as he almost crashed into him. "There is no need to shout we're not all deaf like Grandad you know. You are going to have to be a little bit more responsible when Mum and the new baby come home you know that don't you? Now look you've knocked my coat off the hooks, please hang it back up and then come *slowly* back to the kitchen." There is was the finger wag and the '*more responsible'* line.

"Like clockwork," huffed Tom to himself as he lifted his dad's coat from the floor. About to walk towards the waft of his delicious smelling food Tom stopped. On the floor beneath the coats lay a piece of blue paper.

"Phew that was close, it must have fallen from my pocket," whispered Tom speedily snatching it up. Fumbling in his shorts Tom pulled out a matching piece of blue paper, his piece from the hospital.

Holy smokes!

Chapter 3

Ice Cream Breakfast

"What do you mean there's another one? Slow down and breath before you faint."

Tom popped his head out from beneath the bedcovers to check the coast was still clear and with a gasp of clean air buried himself again.

"A blue Perkins invitation. It was under the coat rack at home. I think it fell from Dads coat when I knocked it off the hook but this one had a phone number scribbled at the bottom."

"I told you," interrupted Sid. "I told you I bet they got one as well. Now you're in trouble Tom they are going to become professional crafty sneaky people at sneaky crafty things. Did you keep the phone number?"

"No I put it back *stupid* or they would know something was up," snapped Tom. "I did remember it but now I've forgotten,

I know it started 24 and I think it ended with a 3 or maybe an 8 or was it a 5?"

"Well I would have taken a photo on my phone, so I did remember it *stupid*," threw back Sid crossly.

"Stop it already will you, did they look suspicious when you were eating?" questioned Ben.

"No, they looked normal like they do every time we eat together. Grandad slurped and spilt his gravy down his chin and top *as always*, Gran told him off *as always* and Dad laughed *as always* before he did the same. Honestly, if it had been me the tutting and napkin wiping would have started not laughing. I just shovelled the food, disguised veggies and all in as fast as I could and made my excuses to leave the table."

"Ah-ha the old camouflaged veg trick hey. They must think we're blind there is no way you can hide green where green simply shouldn't be. Where are they now?" asked Sid.

"Gran and Grandad left a while ago and Dads watching the footie on TV. How could he deny seeing that man when he must have spoken to him to get that paper, what a liar?"

"BEN BEDTIME," Bens mums voice called down the crackly line.

"Got to go," said Ben. "See you at school tomorrow and we can talk then…out."

"Me to, night Tom, see you tomorrow and be careful," said Sid as both radios fell silent.

Tom lay in bed listening to the TV downstairs and Dad shouting his professional opinion at the players as if they could hear him. His mind a jumble of questions he didn't know the answers to, and he knew the grown-ups wouldn't answer if asked he closed his eyes.

Never mind Mum would be home tomorrow with baby William and things would all be back to normal. How wrong could Tom be?

normal

adjective

Conforming to a standard; usual, typical, or expected.

In other words how things used to be before baby William came home!

Whatever this was it certainly was as far from normal as normal could be. No one told Tom that this much would change when a new baby came into the house. His whole world had been turned upside down. Over the last few weeks, Mum and Dad had been either asleep, changing exploding nappies, snapping at each other, cleaning up globs of milky puke or speaking mushy baby talk.

Williams ability to projectile vomit vast distances was astounding so Tom stayed out of range as much as possible. Gran and Grandad came around often to help so the house was always full of preoccupied people meaning Tom had more time to do things he wanted to do without having to be ‘responsible’.

“Yeh I’m sure it’s gone, I’ve not seen it for days now and I have even checked my dad’s coat pocket. They probably chucked it in the bin covered in baby sick or poo like everything else. Anyway, Dad’s back at work today so he can’t be going to some school. Pass me that big nail there,” said Tom pointing with a rather large hammer.

“Aren’t you still curious though?” asked Ben handing him a large rusty nail from their old jam jar supply donated by Sid’s grandpa. “I know I am, and us kids need to know these things. We must stay one step ahead of the parents or all is lost."

"That's a bit dramatic," added Sid with a frown.

"Of course I'm curious, but right now it doesn't involve any of us or our parents. Besides, we have more important things to do like fix this hole in the roof," said Tom holding down a piece of fresh plastic over a startled squirrel shaped hole. "Here Sid hold this nail still whilst I hit it."

"Do I look stupid?" no reply. "Hold it yourself I like my fingers thank you. I'll hold the plastic and get a move on I don't want to waste all morning of our day off school, don't you love teacher training days? Grandpa gave me some money for us to get ice cream in town and I want to get there before they sell out of banana flavoured."

"Sid they will never sell out of banana flavoured as you're the only one crazy enough to eat it. I'm surprised Bella keeps ordering it, its gross I don't know why you like it," said Tom with a thwack of the nail. "There that should do it, now grab those branches and bits, the sooner they are back on top the sooner we can take 'Banana Man' here for his ice cream."

Bella Bellissima's was the place to go for the best ice-cream in town. Opposite the park and next door to the coffee shop its red, white and green sign shone in the morning sunlight like a beacon guiding children to this palace of treats.

“Yummy, ice cream for breakfast thank you Grandpa,” said Sid licking the sweet melting stream of banana flavoured cream off his hand. “Makes up for the fact that *someone* made us meet so early this morning.”

“My mum would never let me do this,” grinned Ben as he loudly slurped a large chunk of chocolate from his sugar cone. “She would go off like a nuclear bomb if she knew.”

“Well they won’t know, will they?” said Tom swinging his denim covered legs from the park climbing frame. “As far as they all know we're still at the den and besides Sid's grandpa won't say anything will he Sid?

"Nah, Mum would nag his ears off, and he would certainly get the 'how could you do that' hands if he did, he's not silly. Besides my mum and dad are both at work today so we're safe."

Slowly the morning sun gained heat and as they enjoyed their ice cream breakfast the carefree boys watched the busy world pass by. Cars carrying people to work, Bella's shop bell tinkling, kids rushing to school that didn't have a teacher training day (unlucky) and the steady flow of people getting their morning coffee and pastries from the coffee shop.

"Didn't you say your dad was back at work today Tom?" crunched Ben on a mouthful of his crispy cone.

"Yep sure is. Secretly I think he's looking forward to the peace. He left early this morning," replied Tom licking sweet strawberry sauce off his thumb.

"So why has he just walked into Pinker's coffee shop?"

"No, you're seeing things, my dad will have been at work ages ago."

"Nope, definitely him," slurped Sid. "Look he's talking to my mum and dad. Hold on a minute they should be at work as well!"

“Curiouser and curiouser,” said Ben as he dropped from the climbing frame and dove for cover behind the park hedge.

Through the leaves and branches, the three watched as Tom’s dad and Sid’s parents chatted whilst patiently waiting their turn in the queue.

“Oh, scary look Ben three people in a coffee shop ordering… wait for it… coffee,” said Sid cheekily as they moved forward and placed their orders.

“Shut up,” hissed Tom, “something isn’t right why are they not at work?”

“Maybe they’re playing hooky and having a day off,” whispered Sid as Ben shoved him over for being daft.

Three tall white cups of hot coffee were placed on the counter and Tom, Ben and Sid watched as the grown-ups walked over to the nearest booth to sit.

“Well they certainly aren’t going to work, are they? If I played hooky from school, I would be in no end of trouble so how come they get away with it?” wailed Ben looking towards Tom. “Tom are you ok, you look a bit odd?”

No Tom wasn’t ok his heart was racing, his throat felt sore and he couldn’t believe his eyes. Standing behind the counter serving their parents coffee was the weasel faced man.

Chapter 4

Two Tall Lattes

"That's him, that's the man from the hospital I told you about," spluttered Tom waving a pointed finger.

"Serving coffee, are you sure?"

"One hundred per cent I'm sure and he knows our parents."

"Speaking of parents where did they go?" asked Sid finishing his ice cream and throwing the tip of his cone away (he never ate that bit, no one asked why it was just a Sid thing). The booth in the coffee shop window was now empty as if their parents had vanished into thin air.

"Did you see them leave, they can't have gone far?" asked Tom standing above the hedge and frantically looking for the familiar sight of Dad.

"Erm, Tom you know that number on the blue paper you saw, it wouldn't be 239713 by any chance would it?" asked Ben.

Tom thought for a moment, "Yes that was it, how do you know?"

Ben pointed to the sign above the window. “Because it’s written there, it’s the coffee shop phone number,” replied Ben as another realisation struck him, “and look Pinkers.”

“I don’t get it,” said Sid confused as always, “what about Pinkers Perks & Beans its always been called that?”

“P-I-N-K-E-R-S,” said Ben, “rearrange it, Sid.”

Sid tried, “NIPERKS, KERPINS, SERKNIP… nope still don’t get it.”

“P-E-R-K-I-N-S,” Ben spelt slowly. “It’s the school, right in front of our faces all this time.”

“*The coffee shop is the school,*” shrieked Tom bolting upright before Ben and Sid dragged him down behind the hedge again.

“No, it can’t be, it’s just a coffee shop watch these people,” said Sid as two ladies walked through the doors leaving their children’s scooters just inside after dropping them at school.

The boys watched the weasel faced man as he served them both a croissant and hot drink and, like Tom and Sid’s parents they walked to the window booth and sat down.

“See they’re just having a coffee and a natter like my mum does. First, they stir their drinks whilst chattering away about all sorts of rubbishy not important mum things, take a sip and then they *disappear!*" exclaimed Sid in shock as the two ladies vanished.

"DID YOU SEE THAT?" screamed Tom in a panic. *"OH MY GOSH, WHERE DID THEY GO?"*

"Shush," snapped Ben, "look it's not only them some of the others do it," as a selection of other customers randomly disappeared in a blink.

"But why only some, why not all of them?" questioned Tom.

"Sneaky strategies," said Sid quietly nodding to himself. "I bet not all of them are parents."

"We need a closer look," insisted Tom as he darted across the road and hid behind a large litter bin outside Bella's.

The sound of the coffee machine hissed and burbled like a hungry monster out of the shop door mingled with the chatter of remaining customers. As a young couple approached Ben gasped.

"I know them, they live near my Aunty Mandy's house and they've just had a baby called Brodie. My mum and dad were only talking to them a couple of days ago."

Focusing on their every move the boys watched as the young couple walked inside and ordered a drink. The suspicious man (as he was forever to be known) walked to the machine and with a methodical flick of switches and a hiss of steam poured two tall lattes before placing them on the counter. Then to the three watchers surprise, he discreetly dropped a small pink tablet into the milky topping.

After a brief conversation, a flash of blue paper and a nervous nod of understanding the young couple sat at a table and began to stir the mugs of hot liquid.

"They're mixing the tablet in," whispered Tom in astonishment. Allowing a moment of cooling time both took an apprehensive sip from their tall white china cups. Another sip followed by a third then *poof!* they vanished into thin air.

As if by magic their two now empty chairs slowly scraped backwards and as the boys watched a door at the back of the shop labelled 'STAFF ONLY' opened seemingly by itself and then closed. Not one person in the shop flinched or even seemed to notice this odd occurrence but the three spectators outside did.

Across the road back to the park in a bundle of panic and shock they did not stop until they were a safe distance away. Neither one spoke for a second as they tried to catch their short shallow breaths and release the panic shaking in their limbs.

"Vanishing pills in their coffee, sneaky little…"

"Sid watch your mouth," said Ben before cupping his hand across his mouth. "Oh no, I sound just like my mum."

"You sound like a Perkins Perfect Parent, that's what you sound like," said Tom, "and we have to get inside that coffee shop."

Chapter 5

The Vacuum of Vengeance

"How on earth are we going to get in there, that creepy coffee man is always at the counter," asked Sid.

"He must need to go the bathroom at some point, we just need to wait," replied Ben. So sneaking closer they sat and watched and waited but the man never left the counter unless it was to clear tables.

"Maybe he's a superhuman called Bladder Man" moaned Sid. "Does he never need to go to the toilet because I sure do?"

After what seemed like an eternity (probably 30 minutes which apparently is an eternity to a 10 year old) a phone finally rang in a back room and the man stepped away to answer it.

"Now's our chance come on," said Tom bolting for the open door without thought or more importantly any kind of plan.

"Tom, hold on what are you doing you'll get caught?" cried Ben running after him followed by faithful Sid who had no clue what was happening.

Once inside Tom stopped and looked around frantically, there were two ladies deep in conversation at the back of the shop by the ‘STAFF ONLY’ door so they couldn’t just barge past them.

Left then right Tom looked desperately for any spark of inspiration as Ben and Sid stumbled around him in alarm.

“He’s coming back quick run,” cried Ben grabbing Toms arm and trying to drag him outside.

“No wait I have an idea,” said Tom dashing to the nearest table and grabbing one of the two half full coffee cups standing there. “Here down this quick,” as he took a giant gulp of the lukewarm milky coffee the young couple had left inside.

"What? No way I hate coffee its vile," said Sid as Ben followed suit and took a big gulp screwing up his face in disgust and sticking out his tongue *Blah!*

As the others began to vanish Sid knew he had no choice and grabbing Toms cup swigged the remainder of the tepid, bitter tasting liquid, milky skin and all. A shudder of utter disgust wriggled down Sid's body, as he watched his hand vanish. Arms, body, legs then feet Sid vanished completely, and not a second too soon as the man reappeared behind the counter.

Stopping he looked around as if sensing something was amiss but after a moments pause, continued with his cleaning. Sid held his breath, too afraid to move, as the man walked to the table next to him and cleared away the empty cups.

"*Psstt* Sid, over here," whispered Tom who along with Ben had magically reappeared before invisible Sid's eyes.

"Blimey I thought we'd had it then," whispered Sid as he followed them to the 'STAFF ONLY' door. The two ladies engrossed in their dose of daily gossip did not bat an eyelid as the wooden floor creaked and the door by their side slowly opened.

The room was surprisingly small with a rather low ceiling and lining two walls were shelves displaying cleaning solutions, soft cloths and freshly laundered napkins.

Along the back wall rested a metal bucket with a well-used old mop propped inside, a red vacuum with a smiley one eyed face that had seen better days and several odd dustpans and brushes. Closing the door softly the three boys squeezed into the enclosed space.

“Now what?” asked Ben looking around and towards the ceiling light at some thick fabric strips that dangled out of place.

"There has to be something," insisted Tom moving random bottles and pushing walls. "They don't come back out again so there has to be another way out somewhere. Help me look."

Ben began to run his hands along the shelves top and bottom feeling for buttons or switches as Tom examined the items stacked on them. Sid started with the mop and bits and pieces on the floor.

"This old thing looks like my mum's Vacuum of Vengeance," said Sid moving aside the sad looking one eyed vacuum.

"What on earth is a Vacuum of Vengeance?" asked Ben almost afraid of the answer.

"You know when you're at that crucial point in a game or a movie or something and your mum just barges in and starts vacuuming in front of you."

"Yeh, or when you're having a lie in and they want you to wake up," added Tom.

"That's the Vacuum of Vengeance, and another thing if I left the light on in a room like this at home, I would get into real trouble for wasting electricity. I can hear them now *we're not made of money Sidney Welbury turn off the light when you leave a room.* I bet they teach that at this Pickles Perfect School."

"Perkins, Sid its *Perkins*," corrected Ben running his hands on the floorboards looking for a trapdoor edge (there had to be a trapdoor, there was always a trapdoor, right?) when Tom gasped.

"Sid you genius," as he reached past crouching Ben and flicked the rather grubby light switch to OFF.

Holding their breath in the pitch black room the boys waited for something, anything to happen. Maybe a secret doorway or maybe the floor was going to dissolve beneath their feet. A clunk below the floorboards followed by a slight shudder signalled 'the something' was happening.

A strange fluttering rose in their tummies as the small room began to descend from the coffee shop above.

"Tom what have you got us into this time?" asked Ben kneeling on the floor as his breath quickened and the hairs on his neck stood to attention. Sid shuffled back into the safety of the one eyed vacuum corner as the lightbulb flickered back into life.

Moving slowly at first the room gradually gained speed before it took off like a startled rabbit. Plummeting down, left then right, forwards and sideways it rushed along to who knows where.

"That will be what those straps are for," wailed Ben pointing to the ceiling as he rocked around on his hands and knees trying desperately to keep his balance. "Adult height handles."

"I didn't know lifts did this or cleaning cupboards to be fair. It's like being on a rollercoaster and to be honest, I wish I hadn't had that banana ice cream now," squealed Sid as the mop crashed to the floor.

With that, there was a sudden bolt forwards knocking the boys to the back of the room before they began to slow down almost to a grinding halt. Gently the cleaning room rose and with a soft jolt and a *DING,* they came to a delicate stop.

"Well Toto I don't think we're under the coffee shop anymore," whispered Ben.

Sid had no idea who Toto was, and he wasn't going to ask for fear of being called stupid again.

"Tom please be careful," he whispered as his friend reached for the handle and with a click, opened the door.

Chapter 6

The Bubble Bath Toilet

Tom slowly pulled the door towards him listening for any signs of life and once he was happy it was safe, he cautiously poked his head out.

"All clear," he whispered back to his partners in crime who followed as he snuck from the room.

The boys stood in a long narrow corridor carpeted in regal blue with crisp white walls and at the far end stood a pair of tall glazed doors guarding the exit. On each glass pane, a large ornate letter ‘P’ stood proudly emblazoned in gold.

“Look ‘P’ for Perkins,” said Tom starting to walk towards them.

“P for *P*erhaps we should go home now,” said Ben turning to look at the relative safety of the cleaning cupboard lift before catching Tom and Sid up.

“Now I know we are not under the coffee shop anymore, look at that,” gasped Sid as they peeped through the glass.

Hanging high above a glistening white marble foyer a magnificent crystal chandelier danced rainbows. A pair of imposing glass doors flanked by equally large windows stood at one side. These looked out towards the most perfect lawn which had been mown in perfect stripes and was so long it disappeared into the perfect pink blossom trees beyond.

Opposite the garden doors stood an impressive semi-circular desk and either side two majestic staircases swept to a vast balcony above.

Lining the walls were several sets of doors mirroring the ones they were hiding behind and inlaid in the cold marble floor, a huge gold circle with three entwined P's glimmered for *P*erkins *P*erfect *P*arents.

"Down," cried Ben snatching the other's arms as a man appeared beyond one of the other doors. Barging them open he dashed into the grand room and towards the desk where a lady perfectly dressed in a formal fitted blue suit and white shirt had appeared.

"Where did she come from?" whispered Tom peeping through the glass, planning to eavesdrop on their conversation.

"Welcome to Perkins how can I help you? Ah, Mr Dawson, you are late today."

"Yes I know I'm so sorry we overslept," said the out of breath man shaking his wet raincoat. "Then the car wouldn't start and when it did, I got stuck in awful traffic. Why they insist on digging the roads up by the station all the time I'll never know. All this new parent lark is really hard work."

"The train station," whispered Ben confused, "but that's miles from our coffee shop and why is his coat wet it wasn't raining."

"He doesn't mean our train station these doors must lead to all the other coffee shops they own. Look there are loads of them and see the name plaques above each one, that must be where they lead to. That man came from Kings Cross Station," replied Tom.

"You're kidding me?" said Sid, "first wizards and now crafty sneaky Perkins Parents. That Kings Cross Station is a dodgy place if you ask me."

"Norwich, Portsmouth, Plymouth, Birmingham, Manchester, Nottingham, Newcastle, Edinburgh, Aberdeen the list goes on," read Ben aghast.

"What does that sign say, the fancy one with red curtains hanging either side?" asked Sid straining his eyes.

"Buckingham Palace," gulped Tom.

"Hang on guys," said Sid, as his mind whirled. "What if they own coffee shops all over the world? Perkins world domination!"

Tom thought for a moment then shook his head. “Don’t be silly Sid, how would people get here from other countries, across oceans?”

“Teleporters,” breathed Sid slowly with a knowing nod. This was answered with an exasperated tut and roll of eyes from Ben any parent would be proud of.

“Well, Mr Dawson if you hurry you will just make the last part of Professor Bumberclap’s lesson on Straight Faces and Flatulence. With a nod of thanks, the man rushed up the stairs two at a time and disappeared from view. Shortly a knock echoed from the balcony above followed by a bellowing “COME IN.”

“Look she’s gone again, how odd,” said Ben staring at the desk where the smartly dressed lady had once stood.

“Never mind her we need to get upstairs and find out what’s happening in those classrooms,” said Tom urgently. “Kid kind is depending on us remember?”

“What’s flatulence?” asked Sid curiously as they crept from the protection of the corridor and into the exposed space of the grand room.

“Farts Sid,” replied Ben. “It’s a posh word for farts, trumps, guff’s, parps, toots whatever you like to call them.”

Sid sniggered as they moved towards the nearest staircase and were about to start climbing when suddenly……

BRRRRIIIIING!… a shrill bell rung and doors above began to open allowing hundreds of adult voices to spill onto the balcony.

The boys sprinted for the nearest hiding place, the giant desk and squashed underneath observing the various strangers faces rushing along the balcony heading for their next lesson.

“Look there’s my dad, what a traitor,” snapped Tom as his dad appeared laughing deep in conversation with a fellow pupil.

Doors opened and closed, and the students began to clear as the halls fell silent.

The boys were about to emerge when all of a sudden, they heard the sound of feet hurrying down the stairs.

"I'm on my way, has he actually been sick? Oh dear well I am in the gym right now, but I'll be with you as fast as I can. Did you try my husband? Ah yes, he's at the training ground so he'll have his phone off sorry. Yes, thank you for calling me, I'll be with you as soon as I can."

A lady dressed in expensive designer gym gear holding a mobile phone in her perfectly manicured hands ran down the stairs and dashed through the doors labelled Manchester.

"Even the footballer's wives are at it, I don't think I will ever trust a grown-up again," exclaimed Ben.

"Here this might help," said Sid holding out a brochure with a map of the school he had found under the desk.

Tom, Ben and Sid could not believe their eyes, the school was like a labyrinth. Room after room floor after floor and corridor after corridor it went on forever.

"Look they have an entire floor dedicated just to Teenager Management," pointed Sid. "A whole floor, what on Earth do they learn in there?"

"I don't think I want to know but it's this area we need to worry about right now," whispered Tom pointing on the map to **Tween Tweaking and Tactics** located on the first floor directly above their heads.

Slipping from the shelter of the desk Tom lead the way as the nervous boys began to climb one of the imposing staircases. Silently they slipped their hands across the polished bannister rail and their trainer covered footsteps were quietened by the thick blue carpet. Arriving at the top first Tom checked the hallway was clear before giving the others the green light.

Left then right they looked at row upon row of doors retaining the muffled sounds of teacher's voices, and shadows moving inside that cast onto the walls beyond.

Slowly they tiptoed to the nearest door and Ben read quietly…

Professor Boris Bumberclap

Straight Faces and Flatulence

Without warning there vibrated the loudest rippling fart noise from beyond the door followed by a sudden burst of giggles and sniggers.

"NO, NO, NEVER LAUGH," came the bellowing voice of presumably Professor Bumberclap. "You must never ever encourage them. Remember F-I-N-F-farting-is-not-funny."

"Oh yes, it is" giggled Sid as he peeped through the glass at neat rows of adults sat at their desks trying not to laugh whilst the small, round, balding man at the front shook his head in disappointment.

Leaving Sid to watch Tom scuttled below the door and read from the next.

Madam Clarissa Countenance

The Face

Inside this room rows of obedient parents were glaring ferociously at a rosy cheeked lady with a mass of curly wild grey hair wearing a pair of large purple glasses.

“Now remember ‘The Face’ says it all when we cannot use words in public places or when we have company present. They need to know that this look means business and to stop whatever they are doing or saying *RIGHT NOW,*” as she slammed her hand violently on the desk.

The class of parents flinched in surprise before going back to pursing their lips tightly together and staring so hard it looked like their eyeballs may drop out of their heads at any moment. This was the price they were willing to pay to perfect the perfect glare.

“I bet my mum got an A+ star in that class,” said Ben. “She’s a pro at ‘The Face’ even my dad says so. When she does that glare, I know I'm in big trouble. It's like her eyes burn into my brain and scream *STOP IT BEN*."

"Well my nan always says if you pull a face and the wind changes, you will stay that way," informed Sid before dropping his shoulders in realisation. "That's another Perkins fib isn't it?"

Disappointed Sid crept like a stalking animal low across the hallway and peeped into another door.

Miss Petunia Pointer
The Finger of Doom

A tall painfully thin lady with a long pointed nose and blonde hair pulled into a ponytail so tight it made her eyes narrow was pointing violently at a student. Her long thin index finger with knobbly knuckles and sharp pink manicured nails was aimed at a gentleman, cowering at the back of the room sat next to Sid's dad.

"*No* Mr Taylor you need to extend your digit much more and make the grip tight. Lock your wrist and don't waggle it so much. A floppy finger never achieved anything."

"Sorry Miss Pointer," said the man, "but I struggle with it, I was always taught pointing is rude."

"It *is* rude Mr Taylor you're right but there is pointing and then there is the 'Finger of Doom'. Without this knowledge and ability, your children will never know you are in charge or that you mean what you say. 'The Finger of Doom' is something every parent should and will master. Now try again and give it a sharp jab when you need to define a word of threat in your sentence."

Mr Taylor nervously cleared his throat and tried again.

"If (jab of a finger) I ever (jab of a finger) find you have poured an entire bottle of bubble bath into the toilet as a science experiment and flushed it again I will ground you (jab of a finger) and (jab of a finger) remove your games controller for a month. I am not joking just you try it and see," (jab and a small wiggle).

"Much better," praised Miss Pointer with a smile. "Three jabs in succession and just enough waggle at the end to drive the point home. Perfect Mr Taylor."

"Now Mr Welbury, your turn let's see if you have been practicing since our last class."

Sid slipped down below the glass, he knew his dad had been practicing all too well.

"They teach them the finger," he whispered to Ben and Tom across the hallway who looked at him in shock.

"What this finger?" asked Ben raising his middle finger rudely and waving it at Sid with a grin.

"No dim whit much worse, this finger," said Sid pointing his best 'Finger of Doom' at them with a shudder.

The adjacent door belonged to

Miss Prunella Polish

Department of Manners

Here a very perfectly dressed spick and span lady was walking between the desks in her high heels. The students were reciting yes *please*, no *thank you* and *excuse me* to the beat of a ticking pendulum.

"Now remember you must correct them instantly on any forgotten manners, never leave a pause as the opportunity will be lost. The only way to teach children true manners is repetition and perseverance until it is drummed into their little minds," Miss Polish instructed.

Projected onto the board a diagram explained how children should never be allowed to interrupt adults when they are speaking whilst covering one wall, a colourful poster instructed on tackling your child when they let out an uncontrollably loud burp in others company.

"Hey that kid on the poster looks like me," said Ben.

"And so it should," replied Tom you are the burp maestro after all. I have never met anyone else that can burp the complete alphabet with such style."

"Yes I am aren't I," said Ben proud of his rare talent as he took a deep throaty gulp and belched out a humongous rippler.

With a laugh caused partly by fear the boys ran and hid up a nearby staircase.

"Was that you Professor Bumberclap?" shouted a rather cross ladies voice as doors flew open.

"No, it wasn't Miss Pointer. May I ask why I always get the blame when a rude sound is projected into these corridors? I do not release flatulence for fun you know," and his door slammed shut hiding the laughter coming from his pupils inside.

When the culprit couldn't be found one by one, the doors closed, and classes continued.

"That was probably my best one yet," said Ben proudly looking up from their hiding place at the steps that vanished into the dark. "Where do you think these go?"

CHAPTER 7

Enter at Your Own Risk!

TEENAGE MANAGEMENT

ENTER AT YOUR OWN RISK!

ACCESS LEVEL 4 STAFF ONLY

Slouch, Slob & Sleep Limitation

Arguments & Victory

Bedroom Monstrosity Management

Hygiene & Hormones Dept

Square Eyes & Social Media Addiction
Insubordination & Insults Deflection
Tug of War & Tantrums
Patience & Perseverance
Understanding the Urban Dictionary
Games Console Dependency

"And there it is the games controller removal lesson, our parents must be on the advanced course," huffed Tom.

"Welcome to the dark side," said Ben in his best deep dramatic movie voice. "Let's go see."

One step was all they took towards the darkness when there was suddenly a loud ear piercing scream followed by the stamping of feet and slamming of a door.

Scurrying down the stairs towards them a lady grasping a handkerchief appeared. She was white as a sheet with dishevelled silver flecked hair and mascara filled tears ran down her makeup stained face.

The boys had no time to hide and instead stiffened in panic as she ran straight past them seemingly oblivious to their presence. In turmoil, her entire body shook, and she kept muttering repeatedly to herself, “I can’t do this, it’s too much their all monsters.”

Down the main staircase, the poor lady fled aiming for the reception below and as her heavy sobs turned into wails a door banged as she made her escape.

"Maybe we should give that floor a miss," said Tom wisely stepping back into the hallway.

With a glance over the balcony checking no one was onto them, they continued along the blue carpeted pathway. Turning a corner they were greeted with the most delicious smell wafting from a room close by.

Madame Cornelia Clandestine Culinary Con and Camouflage

"That smells amazing, I'm starving," moaned ever hungry Sid clutching his tummy as it grumbled back its agreement. The classroom looked much like the ones the boys had at school for cookery lessons, nothing scary there.

Madame Clandestine walked around each workstation guiding groups of parents who were chopping, blending and stirring their marvellous creations.

"Look there's my mum making her famous pizza, I adore Mums homemade pizza," said Sid salivating at the thought.

"Now remember class vegetables and all things healthy can be concealed almost anywhere if you are creative. Bolognese, lasagne, pasta sauces, soups, shepherd's pie, the list is endless. The trick is to mask the taste of the vegetables with stronger flavours like a good dose of garlic, onion, ginger, herbs or tomato. All work equally well I have found from experience."

The class watched as Madame Clandestine took a perfectly ordinary pizza dough base and spread it thickly with some tomato sauce mixture from Sid's mum's bowl before sprinkling on ham and pineapple and a good deep covering of cheese.

"There we have it class, an innocent pizza but hidden in that tomato sauce there are 22, yes 22 different vegetables they will never discover."

"*22 veggies in that one pizza, Mum, how could you*?" screamed Sid at the top of his voice staring at his mum in shock.

"*Shut up Sid*," cried Tom and Ben pulling him from view just as his mum glanced towards the familiar voice.

THUMP, THUMP, THUMP...

loud music started in the room next door and not a moment too soon as it masked Sid's cry of disgust.

"Is everything alright Mrs Welbury?" asked Madame Clandestine following her gaze.

"Erm, yes sorry. It sounds a little crazy, but I could swear I just heard my sons voice. My mistake must have been the music."

Sid was gobsmacked, "22 veggies hidden in one pizza, crafty sneaky good for nothing con-artist's the lot of them.

No more of Mums pizza for me then,
nada, no way, never again."

"I don't think I could even name 22 vegetables," said Tom starting to count on his fingers.

Ben looked at his friends, "Why are you guys so fixated on the veggies, does the idea of pineapple on pizza, not freak you out coz it does me. That's just nasty!"

THUMP, THUMP, THUMP...

the music grew louder drawing the boys curiosity away from the saga of the 22 vegetables.

Multicoloured lights started to flash from the room and into the hallway, bouncing off the three curious faces sneaking towards the door. Inside loud cheers and whoops were accompanied by claps and singing, well if you could call it singing it sounded more like a cat with its tail trapped. The deep crooning sound of various male voices entirely out of tune and singing completely the wrong words crept under the door.

Through the glass, the boys stared in astonishment. This was no ordinary room, oh no it was a mammoth dance hall with hundreds of glitter balls dangling from the high ceiling. Spotlights of all colours flashed and rotated, drenched the room in darting rainbow coloured lights.

The glitter balls sparkled and flashed as the hall full of dancing men threw their best dance moves to the music of their youth and right in the middle was, yes you guessed it, Tom's dad. Embarrassment overload!

Jaxon Jive
Dad Dancing and Cool Crooning

Ben read the sign on the door as the music changed from 80's pop to Drum and Bass. As the beat sped up and the bass pulsed against the door the dads began to move faster trying to copy an agile man dancing between them.

Jaxon Jive was dressed in a silver sparkling tracksuit with glowing white trainers and blue leg warmers. His skin glowed copper from an awful fake tan and a headband held his long, permed and badly bleached hair back.

"That's it just listen to the beat, let it flow through your veins and wiggle those hips gentlemen," Jaxon yelled through his microphone as he thrust his hips around. "Remember to accentuate your moves the aim is to throw your arms around and take up as much of the dance floor as you can. Sing if you want to the louder the better, I say and if you don't know the words just hum or throw anything in, no one will even notice."

"That is something I can never un-see, " groaned Tom mortified beyond belief as the three slid to the floor.

"If I close my eyes, it's still there," wailed Sid. "I think it's scorched into my eyeballs forever. Sorry Tom but your dads a really bad dancer."

"I'm going to be having nightmares for weeks," groaned Ben as a lone cricket chirped and a piece of tumbleweed blew under the door opposite.

Professor Fredrick Flat
Dad Jokes Delivery Department

The ball of dry tumbleweed rolled soundlessly along the hall and come to rest at a lone dark door a distance away from all the others.

“What do you think they teach in there?” whispered Tom.

“Stay here and keep an eye out, I’ll take a look,” said Ben scooting away into the silence of the corridors furthest reach.

The door was grey and faded with tired flaking varnish and the room beyond stood in darkness. Ben felt a little sorry for it standing there all alone.

Thick dust and a layer of heavy cobwebs covered the glass and door handle, this was a room that had not been used in a long time.

“What does it say?” called Tom as loudly as he could over the music.

"Hold on the signs covered in dust, I can't read it," replied Ben as he licked his finger and began to rub at one end. Slowly peeling back the years of dirt he uncovered three words 'Hand of Pain.' Ben stopped in horror, suddenly he didn't feel sorry for it at all.

"Just a cleaning cupboard nothing to worry about," lied Ben as he returned to the others.

"A real one or magic lift one?" asked Sid wishing for a way home.

BRRRRIIIIING!... the end of a class bell rang out again.

"Oh no quick hide," cried Tom in alarm looking around as the pulsing music stopped and the sound of tired feet approached the door.

There was only one option as they dashed for the cobweb covered door and darted inside. Holding their breath they waited as the movers and shakers, cooks and bad joke tellers along with the class cricket called Steve spilt out from their lessons.

"Hurry now to the Great Hall chip chop," clapped Jaxon Jive. "Our wonderful headmistress would like to welcome you all with an assembly," as he sashayed down the hall behind his pupils herding them to join the other classes now cramming into the hallways.

"Oddest cleaning cupboard I've ever seen Ben," said Tom moving a slipper aside as he propped a fallen cane back against the wall before opening the door with a slap of leather belts that were hanging on the back.

"Lock that one on the way out and lose the key."

Ben grabbed the rusty key inside the door and locked it tightly checking the handle before pushing the key back under the door and away forever. No one would ever get into that room again.

"Come on guys let's see this wonderful headmistress in all her glory," said Tom as he ran along the hall in the direction the parents had travelled. Along the halls and maze of twisting corridors, they followed at a safe distance the vast hordes of parents going to meet the gracious leader of Perkins school.

Pressed flat against the wall Tom, Ben and Sid peered around the corner as the last stray pupils entered the Great Hall through a pair of imposing wooden doors.

Professor Bumberclap was bringing up the rear when he stopped without warning. Shaking his head he took a few slow wobbly steps forward.

"Oh no not n-n-now p-p-please," he stammered as he got slower and slower before stopping completely and his arms and head went limp.

"What's he doing?" whispered Tom. "Do you think he's sick?"

Before they had time to think, two men in grey overalls appeared from who knows where and grabbed the Professor one under each arm. Lifting the professor's feet completely off the floor they vanished into a door camouflaged in the hallway.

"Now that's weird," said Ben. "The professor didn't move when they grabbed him, he just hung between them like a rag doll and don't even start me on who the heck those men were."

"This place just gets stranger and stranger," muttered Tom as slowly the three boys crept forward and pushed the hall doors open a crack, releasing the sound of hundreds of excited parents inside.

The sound was almost deafening as they chatted away over each other catching up on gossip and laughing loudly.

"Hundreds of them," Sid gasped, "there must be hundreds, no thousands of grown-ups in there."

Row upon row upon row of seats filled the wooden panelled hall from the stage at the front to the very back of the room. There were mums, dads, grandparents, foster parents, in fact, any parents of any kind and any age. Some were dressed in suits, others in gym wear or casual clothes. Tom, Ben and Sid recognised their local postman sat at the end of a row in his uniform complete with his overfilled bag.

There were others, firemen, nurses, supermarket staff even pilots all dressed in uniform to keep up the pretence of being at work no doubt when they returned home.

The stage was festooned with opulent royal blue velvet curtains lined top and bottom with gold and above them, a large crest with the three golden P's hung to match the reception floor. A lone microphone stood in the centre attached to a lectern waiting patiently for its speech giver to arrive. Behind this, the teachers (along with Professor Bumberclap's empty chair) filled the stage sat neatly in several rows.

"I'm so excited to be here, I heard all about this place from my parents when I had the baby and then when I received my invitation at the hospital, well I could have burst with pride. A Perkins pupil at last," the lady nearest the door said excitedly to an older lady sat next to her.

Tom noticed she looked tired with no makeup and had baby sick stains on her top just like his mum did when his brother had arrived.

As if someone magically switched off the volume the hall fell silent. Tom, Ben and Sid strained their necks to see through the door crack and above the crowds.

Far across the hall, slow rhythmic footsteps echoed around the enormous room as a pair of towering slender heels approached the stage.

Heads wiggled side to side trying desperately to see through or over the people in front as everyone tried to catch a glimpse of the legendary wearer. The click-clack of heels paused for a moment before one by one they climbed the wooden staircase to the stage.

Chapter 8

A Duck Walked into a Bar!

From beyond the sea of parents, the top of a head appeared rising towards the stage.

“Ouch, get off your pulling my hair,” snapped Tom as Sid scrambled up him trying to see.

Gradually the infamous headmistress Miss Patricia P. Perkins appeared on the stage. Tall and slender with a sharply chiselled nose and chin she approached the lectern.

Her hair was styled in a perfect silver bun without a single strand out of place. Dressed in a royal blue fitted jacket and skirt her pale blue shirt collar lay perfectly upon the lapels.

A string of perfectly simple blue pearls hung around her neck matched with earrings and upon her rather large feet a pair of towering heels made her long legs look even longer. Golden cat-eye framed glasses swayed on a delicate chain and proudly glinting on her lapel was a gold brooch made from the three Ps.

“Wow, she looks mean?” whispered Sid as the others nodded.

“Look at the teachers,” added Tom, “somethings wrong, they aren’t moving and look how they’re staring at the parents.” Even the ever active Jaxon Jive was motionless.

The headmistress took her place behind the lectern. Anticipating silence continued as she placed her glasses delicately on her nose and with a faint clearing of her throat addressed her army of devoted followers.

“Welcome parents new and old to Perkins School,” she announced in a voice so loud it cut the air like a knife making the boys ears ring.

"Here at Perkins, we pride ourselves on being the backbone of perfect parenting life. Child manipulation and educating you as parents to Perkins standards is our primary goal. As you know our teaching methods have been tried and trusted over countless years and have been used on both royalty and unruly Prime Ministers.

Perkins school proudly upholds a flawless reputation and we expect every one of you to put your very utmost into learning our strategies and techniques to control and mould your children into model Perkins citizens.

Do not think it will be easy, and at times it will feel unachievable, but these standards are a necessity for all children. If they were allowed to run free with their lives, I dread to think about what type of society we would live in today.

As parents, grandparents and teachers we have to work united towards one ultimate goal, to be in total command and rule our way. As always please remember, Perkins schools existence must remain a closely guarded secret, and never forget how privileged you are to have been invited to learn our knowledge and skills.

When you became a parent you accepted a great responsibility, to control, discipline, and embarrass your children at every given opportunity.

They will never thank you for it, they will rebel and try your very patience, but we must not weaken. We will never give in to their puppy dog eyes, crocodile tears and trickery to manipulate our adult minds.

A Perkins parent is a strong parent with Perkins blue pride flowing through their veins and we will be *VICTORIOUS*."

As the deafening applause rang out from the freshly inspired grown-ups the three terrified boys made a run for it. Flying down the reception staircase they leapt over poor Steve the cricket from the dad's joke lesson.

"Please take me with you," Steve pleaded in desperation. "I can't stand it here one more day my legs are almost worn through from all those awful jokes."

"Cool a talking cricket," cried Sid. Scooping Steve up he popped him into the safety of his T-shirt pocket.

Tom, Ben and Sid slammed through the 'P' emblazoned doors sending them crashing into the walls. Their throat's raw from shortness of breath the boys and grateful Steve piled into the cleaning cupboard lift and slammed the door shut before hastily flicking the light switch to ON.

The lift kicked into life and took off back towards the coffee shop. Without a word Tom, Ben and Sid held onto anything they could to steady themselves from the rocky ride until the room arrived at its destination with a *ping!*

Taking a deep breath Tom was about to throw the door open and make a break for it across the possibly packed coffee shop when Ben stopped him.

"*Where did that come from*?"

A door had appeared in the wall behind the old mop and bucket at the back of the room (the old secret door trick, should have known it when there wasn't a trap door). Sid stumbled backwards in surprise tripping over the poor Vacuum of Vengeance.

"That wasn't there a moment ago I was leaning on that wall holding on for dear life."

"We need to get out of here," said Tom in a fluster as he grabbed the mop and bucket sending it crashing to the floor. With a twist of the smooth finger worn handle the door opened, and the three boys stumbled out into the tiny passageway behind the shop.

As the doorway faded back into the brickwork, they fled tumbling over the shops metal rubbish bins sending them smashing into the ground.

Scrambling to their feet they ran down the narrow passageway shooting out into the bustling street where they'd stood only a short time before.

A glimpse through Pinker's Perks and Beans window showed the weasel faced man rushing to investigate the clattering noise in his guarded cupboard.

"WHAT ARE WE GOING TO DO?" screeched Ben as they reached the park and grabbing their bikes from the twisted heap, they had abandoned them in pedalled at top speed for the safety of Den Pippin.

Tom didn't answer he was getting as far as he could from anyone that had anything to do with that school. Closing the den door the three panic exhausted and shocked boys collapsed in a puffing heap.

"*WHAT ARE WE GOING TO DO?*" screeched Ben again. "It's like a military training camp for mean parents and they all love her. I knew parents couldn't be that mean naturally."

"Did you see how many grow-ups were there?" asked Sid gently placing Steve the cricket on the den floor. " Kings and Queens and important people like that she said, no one's safe not anywhere."

"You're right Sid. If our grandparents are going it's been around as long as they have if not before. Grandparents, great grandparents even great-great-grandparents this could have been happening for hundreds of years. So how old does that make her?"

"Now boys you should never ask a lady her age it's not polite," said Steve straightening his bow tie. "All I will say is that she's as old as time."

Then with a chirp of thanks, Steve hopped away through a tiny hole in the carpet wall to freedom.

"A talking cricket, cool," muttered Tom. "One thing is for sure, I knew my dad couldn't be that bad a dancer or joke teller without training."

"At least we didn't find the 'Pull my Finger' class, my dad's bound to have been in there showing off his talent. I have never met anyone that can clear a room like him," laughed Sid.

"Guys this is serious," wailed Ben, "quit messing around we need to stop them before it gets out of hand and our parents are mean forever. Remember kid kind is depending on us and is no one else shocked that was a talking cricket?"

"What exactly do you think we can do?" asked Sid. "We can't just walk in there and say *excuse me we hear you're teaching parents to be mean to us kids so please stop it.*"

Tom sat quietly listening to the others argue, deep in his stomach he had an awful feeling like a giant knot turning tighter with every thought. What had happened to poor Professor Bumberclap and why did all the teachers look so odd on the stage?

Who were the men in the grey overalls and where did the lady behind the desk appear from and vanish to? What was this place and what were they going to do to stop it?

That evening Tom watched his parents closer than usual, he didn't hide away in his room, instead, he watched and listened for the clues.

Dad was cooking as usual due to Mum being a rubbish cook, her bread rolls had been used for cricket practice many a time. The radio was playing away softly in the background when a song came that made Dad reach for the volume button.

He started to wiggle his hips whilst stirring his famous Bolognese Surprise that he had successfully hidden countless yucky vegetables in (all 22 of them).

He then began to dance on the spot singing into the wooden spoon at Mum who was watching and laughing. As a finale, Dad launched himself around the kitchen table in full Jaxon Jive groover mode.

Did he know the words? No!

Did he think he looked cool? Yes, he did much to Toms embarrassment.

The Face, The Finger of Doom and correction of every missing please and thank you all made an appearance as unfortunately did the appalling Dad jokes.

"Hey, Tom did you hear about the duck in the bar?"

"No Dad" sighed Tom politely having heard this joke a million times.

Brace yourselves this is a side splitter…

"So a Duck walks into a bar and asks got any bread?" Dad started to chuckle, and this was only the first line.

"No replied the barman.

Got any bread? asked the duck again.

No repeated the barman.

Got any bread? asked the duck a third time.

No...and if you ask me again, I'll nail your beak to the bar said the barman."

At this point Dad started to laugh, not just a giggle but a full belly laugh that turned his face red and tears flowed down his cheeks. Finally, the stunning punchline was delivered, are you ready?

"Got any nails? asked the duck. No replied the barman and the duck said got any bread?"

Ta-da (cue tumbleweed)

"Sorry love but I don't get it," said Mum with a perplexed look on her face. Tom continued to tuck into his plate of hidden veg Bolognese whilst his dad howled with laughter and his mum ignored him. Who knew a duck could be so funny!

Dad meanwhile was on a role reeling out his complete repertoire of horrendous jokes that left him with tears running down his face and poor Mum more and more bamboozled.

Tom was horrified, where was Steve the cricket when you needed him?

Looking at William sat on his mum's lap with milk dribbling down his chin Tom decided enough was enough. Using the old faithful homework excuse he left after he had finished eating and hid in his room.

"Sid, Ben are you there? …over."

"*My parents are Perkins parents,*" wailed Bens distraught voice down the crackly radio. "We have to do something if I hear another awful joke or get corrected on a forgotten please or thankyou I'll explode and end up telling them we know their secret."

"They're all Perkins Parents Ben, so what are we going to do, and you forgot to say over," corrected Sid only adding to poor Bens annoyance.

There was a thinking pause from Tom. "We have to go back inside, see what's happening. Something wasn't right with those teachers."

"You're joking right?" asked Sid before realising by the lack of reply Tom wasn't.

"Not when there are people around though, it's too risky the parents or teachers might see us. We have to go in when schools finished for the day and everyone has left."

"You have a plan, already worked out, don't you?"

"Of course."

"I don't like the sound of that," mumbled Sid.

"Over."

Chapter 9

Moist Chocolatey Cupcakes

“So are we clear?” asked Tom looking at the others slowly demolishing the packet of sweets Sid’s grandpa had given them as they passed through the farm to Den Pippin.

“Yes, boss all clear,” slopped Sid as he tongue wrestled a particular chewy toffee jammed around his back molar. “My parents won’t mind me stopping at yours for a sleepover, they never do.”

“No mine neither,” added Ben. “They’re happy for the peace so it won’t be a problem as long as they don’t find out or else the Perkins Perfect Parent class on ‘How to explode at Ben like a nuclear bomb of madness’ will be launched.

“Do they have that class?” asked Sid stopping his toffee battle and looking awfully worried.

“No Sid,” tutted Tom but maybe they should have a ‘Slap Sid when he’s being Stupid’ class. I would go to that one.”

“Well there’s no need to be rude,” grumbled Sid returning his tongue to the offending sweet.

And so a plan was hatched and on returning home the three boys put the wheels in motion. It was simple Tom and Ben were staying at Sid’s for the night and Sid was staying at Bens as far as their parents knew. Fooling the parents was the easy part the rest was a little trickier.

“Are you sure he’s lazy?” questioned Ben as they watched the man in the coffee shop mopping the floor and wiping down the tables before putting the chairs tidily away.

"Just watch," said Tom with his fingers crossed. Truth be told no he wasn't sure, but he hoped so as his plan depended on it.

The man switched off the coffee machine and turned off the lights in the backroom before his last job, emptying the rubbish.

"Let's go," said Tom as they scurried across the street and down the alley that led behind the shop. Holding their breath in hope they watched and waited.

With a clinking sound, a small swirl of dust appeared from the brick wall behind the cleaning cupboard. They watched as the man stepped out and tossed the rubbish bags into the waiting bins.

"See he is lazy, I told you he wouldn't walk all the way around," whispered Tom with relief as the man moved back inside.

The instant his foot vanished the boys made a dash for the door and watched the man walk back into the shop pushing the cleaning cupboard door closed behind him.

Crackling brickwork and a cloud of falling dust signalled the door blending back into hiding and as the boys landed inside the cleaning cupboard lift the door faded away.

Holding their breath, they listed to the man in the shop as he closed the blinds and the strip of light below the door went out. With a jingling of keys, he locked the front door and the silence signalled to the hidden boys he had gone for the evening.

Reaching for the light switch Tom was about to flick it OFF so the lift would move when Sid interrupted.

"Hold on a second" and pushed past Tom opening the door to the shop.

"What are you doing?" hissed Tom as he watched Sid creep across the freshly mopped floor heading for the counter.

"I'm starving I'll just be a moment," he whispered as his eyes fixed determinedly on the moist chocolatey cupcakes calling to him from under a sparkling glass dome.

Reaching over he carefully lifted the lid with a ding of glass on the plate base and removed the biggest one. Prize in hand

Sid went to return the cover when he looked up, something caught his eye.

Sitting on a chair staring directly at him from beyond the open backroom door was the silhouette of the weasel faced man.

With a clattering of glass, Sid dropped the dome lid clumsily back onto the base and turned to run but wait a moment. Why wasn't the man moving he must have seen him?

"Sid what are you doing, come on," snapped Tom holding the cupboard door open for his annoying ever-hungry friend.

"Just a second," replied Sid holding up a finger as he looked at the motionless man sat in the dark.

Like the pulse of a heartbeat, a tiny blue light flickered on and off somewhere behind his head casting a light into the dark room. The blue glow reflected onto a thin cable that appeared from the man's neck and lead into a dark box beneath his seat.

"Freaky," whispered Sid mesmerised when suddenly the man's head slumped forward. Sid decided he had seen enough and grasping his prized cupcake in his shaking hand dashed back to his partners in crime.

"What do you mean he's still in there?" said Tom as Sid charged into the small room flicking the light switch as he passed.

Bouncing around like pinballs in a machine Tom and Ben listened to Sid trying desperately to get the jumbled words from his terrified mind out of his mouth. It didn't help he was doing this whilst shovelling in the gooey chocolate cupcake.

"Sid stop for a moment you're not making sense," said Tom as the lift stopped with a *ding* to signal its arrival at Perkins School. "What do you mean he was plugged into a box?"

"He was, he was," puffed Sid wiping his chocolate covered lips along his sleeve. "He was plugged into a black box below his seat from a cable in the back of his neck and he didn't move or see me. It was like he was dead or something."

"Or not human," gasped Ben.

"Zombies," gulped Sid.

The three boys looked at each other, nothing made sense in this secret world they had discovered. They had questions, lots of them and there was only one way to find the answers.

With a click, the handle turned, and the door creaked opened revealing the familiar blue carpet. Darkness shrouded them as they crept towards the glass doors leading to the marble reception.

The school was eerily silent, so quiet that Tom could hear his heart pumping in his ears as they pushed open the doors and tiptoed across the cold white floor.

"Welcome to Perkins, how may I help you?" echoed the very correctly spoken loud female voice.

Tom, Ben and Sid froze before rolling their eyes towards the lady now stood behind the reception desk.

"It's her again, where did she come from?" whispered Sid from the side of his mouth.

"Don't say anything," instructed Ben.

The lady looked at them with a fixed almost fake smile for a moment, seemingly waiting for a reply before she unexpectedly flickered. The three boys could see straight through her as she flickered once more then vanished.

“What the…?” said Ben as he and the others dashed towards the desk. Glowing with faint blue light a small black disk lay on the floor between Bens feet.

“Hologram,” gasped Tom, “that’s how she appears and disappears. She must be motion sensitive.”

To test this theory Sid took a few steps back and threw some impressive Dad dance moves impersonating Jaxon Jive. A bright blue flicker came from the disk before she exploded from beneath unsuspecting Bens feet.

“Welcome to Perkins, how may I help you?” the lady appeared with her fake smile and Ben standing inside her body.

Sid tried not to laugh as they stood and waited patiently for her to vanish before a freaked out red faced Ben turned giving Sid a look Madam Clarissa Countenance would be proud of.

“Ben grab one of those maps we’ll need one,” instructed Tom trying to save Sid from a pounding.

Ben did as he was asked and reaching behind the desk, he grabbed a map before joining the others who were already halfway up the stairs.

A glancing blow to the back of Sid's head with the glossy paper made Ben feel much better as he passed the map to Tom.

"Well-well- welcome to Perkins, how may I help you?" sounded in the foyer below.

"She's getting annoying now," said Tom through clenched teeth as they reached the top step.

"So what's the plan?" asked Sid looking to Tom, this was his plan after all. Tom thought for a moment feeling uneasy. The old building cracked, creaked and groaned in far off rooms and corridors almost as if it were breathing, watching their every move.

"That evil woman Miss Perkins office is a good a place to start as any," said Tom pointing to a room labelled 'Headmistress's Office' a few floors above. "If anywhere holds some answers it's got to be there."

Map in hand they set off along the dimly lit corridors, passing room after room in darkness when suddenly Tom stopped at the bottom of a familiar staircase. Double checking the map Tom turned towards the others.

"Oh, no way," exclaimed Sid and Ben in unison.

"It's the fastest way to the office according to this, come on how bad can it be?" he reassured them trying his best to hide the wavering dread in his own voice.

Tentatively one step at a time they climbed the wide creaking stairs into the unknown darkness beyond.

Chapter 10

Stinky Sock Bombs

The further they climbed the heavier the dank air smelt of old socks mixed with rancid mouldy food. The carpet became sticky underfoot and a thick layer of dust began to coat the handrail.

"Oh that pongs," moaned Ben grabbing his nose, "what is that awful smell?"

"Essence of teenager," replied Tom as he pinched his nostrils and blinked his stinging watery eyes. "They must get parents immune to it by being forced to breathe the air whilst they learn."

"No guys look, it's coming from over there," said Sid running to a door that was ajar nearby.

"The cleaners have left the door open on **Bedroom Monstrosity Management**," he read before peering inside and realising how wrong he was, there had certainly not been any cleaners in here for a long time.

This was a move Sid quickly came to regret. The pungent pong billowing from the door was unlike anything Sid had ever experienced before, not even on his grandpa's farm. Sid's colour faded to a sickly shade of pale green before he staggered a little and slammed the door shut.

"Sid are you ok, what was inside?" asked Ben rushing towards his faint friend.

"I don't want to talk about it," groaned Sid gasping for air. "I am never having kids if that's what they create," he retched sliding to the floor to wait for the heavy bitter smell trapped in his nostrils and mouth to fade away.

The stained corridor walls were littered with holes of various shapes and sizes mostly outside the rooms marked **Arguments and Victory** and **Games Console Dependency**. Tom ran his fingers around one just above his head that was shaped exactly like his games controller at home before pulling out a control knob embedded in the plaster.

"Sid get up, we need to get out of here," urged Tom as Sid staggered to his feet before both boys stopped.

A shuffling sound far-off along the hallway drew their attention to an approaching figure. Dashing inside the nearest door the three hid and watched a large portly gentleman with manic white hair and a wiry moustache approach. He wore a tweed suit with a red bow tie that matched his ruddy vein lined cheeks and brown brogue shoes the size of small canoes stuck to the soiled sticky carpets. Staring straight ahead with vacant eyes he shuffled along, shoulders hanging low.

"What is he saying?" whispered Ben as the man grew closer.

"Never surrender, never surrender, *LOL*." The final *LOL* was screamed out loud followed by a screeching laugh and nervous twitch of his head before he started repeating the entire thing. The odd teacher sauntered along the hallway and out of sight.

“Well that’s not freaky at all,” murmured Sid.

“Come on let’s get out of here before someone else comes,” said Tom opening the door followed by Ben.

“Guys what’s a *dingleberry?” asked Sid curiously as he pulled the door labelled **Understanding the Urban Dictionary** closed behind them. Map in hand and ignoring Sid’s bizarre question they headed in the direction the slightly zany teacher had gone.

Little by little the carpet became less sticky and the walls appeared cleaner, the fusty air vanished, and the oppressive feeling of constant doom and gloom lifted.

Pushing through a pair of corridor blocking doors the boys were hit slap in the face by an overpowering smell of lavender, strong perfume and talcum powder. They coughed loudly as the sweet smell filled their lungs.

"Oh, that smells like my granny" wailed Ben wafting the air as he turned to the sign on the overly pink flowery walls.

"**Perkins Perfect Pensioners**, I thought so it's the oldies department."

The plush deep pile pink carpet bounced beneath their feet and racks full of cosy slippers stood by the classroom doors ready for the ageing pupil's return.

Doors were polished to within an inch of their lives and twee paintings of landscapes, puppies and flowers lined the walls. It was a stark contrast to the department they had left behind.

Each classroom door was labelled with extra-large text so the oldies could read them.

Madam Coleen Cringeworthy

Sloppy Kisses & Finger Licking

Sid squirmed in disgust. His nan's kisses were the wettest around and she always licked her wrinkled finger to wipe food smidgens from his face.

Professor Maurice Mute

Hearing Aid Adjustment & Selective Deafness

Professor Hilda Houdini Sweet Snaffling & Evidence Extinguishing

Tom's face broke into a large grin thinking back to the hospital and all those greasy takeaways and chocolate bars he and Grandad had shared when his gran wasn't around. Grandad always said that it was his prerogative as a grandparent to spoil his grandson, but he had to admit the training sure had Gran fooled.

The door labelled **Modern Technology for Beginners** made Ben laugh out loud.

"Oh my grandparents need to join this one, they can't even use a Sky remote or a cash machine never mind texting or the internet. Granny says it's all like a foreign language to them and it's too painful when I try to explain, so I've given up."

"Well we know my nan comes to this one," said Sid pointing at the last door.

Miss Molly C. Oddle

Toddler Talk for Tweens & Teens

"If my nan calls me petal one more time, I swear I'll die of embarrassment."

Tom and Ben laughed, they had seen Sid turn various shades of crimson when his nan was with him, she ruffled his hair and pinched his cheeks before talking to him like he was a 4 year old.

Tom studied the map, “I think it’s just through those doors her office should be at the top of the next staircase.”

Leaving the ‘Oldies Zone’ with a final waft of lavender mixed with a hint of toffee from a subtly placed air fresher, they approached the looming staircase and the solitary door at the top.

A blue carpet pathway led them towards the room with its warm light glowing through the narrow glass pane above the heavy mahogany door.

Ears pressed against the polished wood they listened to the ticking of a clock within and for any sounds of movement from its resident.

Suddenly a flash of shadow ran across the gap under the door. The boys stumbled back in shock and surprise, someone or something was inside.

With a rather miffed Ben on all fours, Tom clambered onto his back and stood full stretch reaching for the glass, but he couldn't quite see. It was so annoying being 10 and short, where was this growth spurt his dad kept saying would happen as he could sure use it now.

"*Psst,*" Sid tapped his shoulders.

Tom hesitated as his brain ran through all the injury scenarios, he could have sitting on Sid's wide farmer's shoulders.

With a brilliant example of 'The Face,' Sid glared impatiently at Tom and patted his shoulders again before crouching down by a wall so Tom could climb onboard.

Dropping from a relieved Bens back, Tom swung his leg over Sid's right shoulder as Sid braced himself against the wall. It was not an elegant sight believe me.

Caught off balance Tom grabbed a handful of Sid's hair to lift his left leg into place. Poor Sid pulled a face like he was chewing a wasp as fat tears welled in his agony filled eyes.

Terrified but in place Tom sat precariously on Sid's shoulders, hair still in hand as Ben helped him to his feet.

One step then another the mighty Sid staggered like a weightlifter under a record breaking load to the door whilst Tom hung on for dear life.

"Smile," *Flash*! Bens phone captured the moment forever. Who knows when a picture of your best friends in a predicament like this could come in useful?

"Put that away," snapped Tom as he reached out his hands and propped himself against the door peeking through the glass.

Miss Perkins office was surprisingly cosy. A warm table lamp glowed as it shone across the room lighting up the bookcase lined walls, all bursting with interesting whatnots and leather bound encyclopaedias. Thick curtains masked the windows and, in the centre, stood a large desk neatly arranged under the light of a brass desk lamp.

Sid swayed under Toms weight. "Hurry up is she there or not?" he griped through clenched teeth to his boney bottomed friend. "I'm about to drop you, you're not as light as you look you know."

Tom looked at the impressive green leather chair behind the desk. That was strange, left then right it appeared to swivel a minuscule amount but was it moving or was it just his tired imagination?

Tom quickly discovered the answer as a large ginger tom cat appeared from behind the desk and launched itself at the door with a hiss and a yowl.

Taken by surprise Tom lurched backwards on Sid's weary shoulders catching both Sid and Ben completely off guard. Sid toppled back as Tom lost his balance grabbing Ben as they fell, and they landed in a tangled heap.

From below the door, the large feline growled as its shadow paced back and forth.

Sid rubbed his head where Tom's foot had kicked him. "Has she got a tiger in there?"

"No it's just a flaming cat," replied Tom untwining his legs from Bens with a groan, "but it's a mean looking sucker."

"A guard cat that's a new one on me," moaned a sore Ben as he got to his feet.

Tom winced nursing his bruised elbow. "How are we going to get in there with that wicked thing inside, it'll claw our eyes out if we open that door."

Sid's eyes lit up, "I'll be back," he said in his best Terminator impression as he vanished down the stairs back towards **Perkins Perfect Pensioners**.

"I'm not even going to ask where he's going," murmured Ben.

He and Tom had learnt years ago not to try, even for the slightest moment, to understand what happened in Sid's marvellous mind. Planet Sid was a crazy world unto its own and a scary place to be.

Eventually, Sid reappeared at the bottom of the stairs.

"Stand aside," he called, "and if I were you, I'd cover my nose." He dashed up the stairs two at a time holding something out arm's length in front of him.

The putrid stench reached the others well before Sid making them gag and clasp their noses in both hands.

Tight in Sid's sleeve covered hand wriggled something that resembled an old battered sock. Well, that's what Tom thought it was, it was hard to tell as it was covered in green mould, fluff and crusty bits of dried food.

"*Open the door now,*" commanded Sid as he reached them. Ben grabbed the handle opening the door a crack as Sid launched the sock into the room and slammed the door shut.

"Where did you get that?" choked Tom.

"Courtesy of **Bedroom Monstrosity Management** and no I still don't want to talk about it," spluttered Sid holding the door closed in case the sock tried to escape.

The yowl from inside was eardrum shattering. Objects crashed to the floor and there was the occasional forceful thump against the door as the putrid sock and the cat went to war.

A small pink nose appeared in the door gap desperately gasping for clean air as the essence of teenager's sock consumed the office. With one last wheeze and dragging of frantic claws, the nose withdrew, and all went quiet.

"Do you think it's dead?" asked Ben putting a cautious ear to the door.

"No my guess is just knocked out, lethal things teenager's socks," replied Sid slowly opening the door and stepping back to let the intense stench escape from the room. Like a wild animal the stinking sock crawled from the room and speed down the hallway returning to the safety of the department it called home.

Chapter 11

Mr Purrkins

Under the soft light of Miss Perkins office, the boys looked upon the giant ginger cat. The air was speckled with drifting auburn hair strands as the ferocious feline lay flat on its back in the centre of the desk, its remaining hair stood on end. All four legs were sprawled out sideways and its pink rasping tongue vibrated on its lips as it gasped for breath. It was alive phew!

Tom gave it an apprehensive poke to make sure it was well and truly out for the count before rather awkwardly picking the large furry beast up and placing it on its bed by the radiator. Hanging from its blue sparkling collar the odd shaped name tag caught his eye.

"Hmm, Mr Purrkins, what a surprise."

With a little leg adjustment and hair smoothing poor Mr Purrkins looked like he had simply fallen asleep, no one would ever know.

Returning knocked over pictures from the desk and standing the poleaxed chair back in place the boys looked around the headmistress's office.

"What exactly are we looking for?" asked Ben scanning the encyclopaedia filled bookcases.

"I have no idea," admitted Tom looking through the papers on Miss Perkins desk. "Anything odd or out of place or even written down. There has to be something in here that tells us what's going on."

Sid started rummaging through the immaculate desk drawers whilst Ben pulled on various books and moved ornaments looking for a secret hidden door. After all, that was what they did in the movies right? If there wasn't a trapdoor there was *always* a secret door.

The suspicious man's cleaning cupboard proved that theory.

"Nothing," said Tom in disappointment slamming the last piece of paper back on the desk pile. "How can there be nothing here?"

"Just a thought but there may be something in there," said Sid's muffled voice from inside a particularly deep desk drawer.

Sid's grubby finger was pointing at a large floor to ceiling curtain matching the others around the room, but this one had a glimpse of door handle peeping from one side.

"Why have you only just thought to mention that?" snapped Tom but he stopped dead hearing the sound of creaking stairs outside. Footsteps approached, a pair of high heels were walking along the hall towards the room.

In a blind panic, Tom and Ben shot under the desk into the cramped foot space, holding in their arms and legs as tightly as they could. Sid, on the other hand, made a dart for the safest place in his mind, yes you guessed it, the large curtain covering the hidden door. Silly Sid!

The footsteps stopped and the door wafted open as Miss Perkins entered her office. Tom could see Sid's grimy grass stained trainers poking from beneath the curtain as he held his breath.

Papers tapped on the desktop as she tidied the pile Tom had been raving through just moments before and a picture frame slid back into its correct spot.

"What have you been doing in here Mr Purrkins, and what is that dreadful odour. I believe you need a bath, my furry friend," Miss Perkins said looking at the sleeping ginger cat. "Well that will have to wait until tomorrow, right now I need to prepare for Monday mornings lessons."

Tom and Ben watched as the pair of perfect high heels walked to the cat bed and a long fingered hand reached down, turning the blue sparkly collar until the name tag appeared. With a click, she delicately removed it from its ring holder.

"What no hello? I guess doing nothing all day is truly exhausting for a cat," as she scratched the sleeping moggies head with her long red nails.

Tom and Ben watched in horror as her feet turned and strode across the room heading straight for the curtain hiding Sid.

With a determined *whoosh*, she pulled the large curtain aside and every muscle in Toms body tightened as he waited for her shriek of discovery.

Ben flicked him a kick and he turned to see the heavy curtain bundled up to one side with the tips of Sid's trainers peeping out. Only Sid could be that lucky.

They watched as the devious headmistress pushed the name tag into the lock and turned until a faint click signalled the door was open, as it closed behind her Sid's face peeped out. *O…M….G….* he mouthed looking at the others who were frantically signalling him to stay put.

Eventually, the sound of metal drawers opening and closing stopped and the door opened. Carrying a large box Miss Perkins proceeded to lock the door and return the key to its sleeping owner.

"I'll see you in the morning lazy bones, sleep well," and with a brisk walk marched from the room.

With her footsteps disappearing Tom launched himself from under the desk.

"Come on," he cried as he opened the door and the others followed.

Keeping a safe distance they shadowed Miss Perkins along the twisting corridors until she turned into a door marked STAFF ROOM. A light flickered on and her shadow from beyond the door vanished deep inside.

Peering through the glass the boys stared open mouthed in amazement. The room was lined with chairs, lots of chairs. Row upon row that filled the entire space like a packed waiting room or a train station.

Each chair had a Perkins teacher sat upon it, some of them the boys recognised like the man muttering to himself in the Teenager Department or from encounters on their first visit.

"There are so many of them," whispered Ben in shock as they watched Miss Perkins wandering between them all resembling a prison guard.

"Why aren't they moving or speaking to her? Why are they still here don't they have homes to go to and families?"

A joining door opened and two men in grey overalls appeared carrying a lifeless Professor Bumberclap under the arms. Placing him in an empty chair one reached behind and plugged a cable in whilst the other twiddled a screwdriver in the poor professors left ear.

Instantly Professor Bumberclap sat bolt upright his eyes fixed forward like an electric shock was running through his entire body. After a short conversation with Miss Perkins and some pointing at the professor the two men left.

Suddenly Sid piped up, “They look just like that man in the coffee shop, the guy who you saw at the hospital Tom, he was sat there just like them I told you so. See the blue lights? He had them and the black box.”

True enough below each chair was a black box with a long cable running to a blue light that flickered on each teacher's neck.

They watched as Miss Perkins carefully went to each teacher in turn, taking something from the box she carried and sliding it into the black box beneath their chair. As she did the blue light flickered faster and faster.

"What is she doing and what are those things she keeps taking from that box?" wondered Tom aloud. "Well, she said goodnight to her beloved cat, so my guess is she isn't planning on going back to her office tonight, let's go and see what's in that room, shall we?"

Leaving her to, whatever she was doing the boys hurried back to the office as fast as they could.

Mr Purrkins was still flat out which made getting the key easy pickings. Tom pushed the key into the lock and turned the handle.

"Well I wasn't expecting that it looks like a bank vault," said Ben as they walked into a small room brightly lit by a single overhead light with no windows.

Both sides were lined with huge metal cabinets full of drawers and at the end stood a single desk with the oldest computer they had ever seen. They only knew it was a computer as they had seen pictures in school lessons. The monitor was the size of a large building brick and tainted yellow from age, underneath it was a box just like the ones in the staff room and the coffee shop.

"I wonder what they mean?" pondered Sid pointing to the words 'NEVER' above the left side cabinet and 'FOREVER' written above the right side.

"Sid keep an eye out," instructed Tom, "and watch that devil cat doesn't wake up."

"What do I do if he does?"

"Take your sock off and wave it at him, it's almost as bad as that teenagers one," grinned Ben.

"Oh stop my side will burst with laughter," muttered Sid unimpressed as he vanished back into the office.

"There are so many drawers," said Ben as he grabbed the nearest one to him and pulled. The drawer slid back effortlessly catching him a little off guard.

"Professor Bumberclap," he read aloud from the label inside. "Tom, look at this its crammed full of those old floppy disks like the ones Miss Foster showed us in school."

"Floppy disks," said Tom surprised, "wow this school must have been around since the dark ages or even before my grandparents. Who still uses floppy disks they belong in a museum?"

Ben removed a disk from the right hand row and looked at Tom a little confused as what to do with it.

“Here put in here,” pointed Tom walking to the desk and the slot in the box beneath the monitor.

The box began to whir, and the screen crackled like a heavy snowstorm before exploding into life. A man appeared presenting an ancient black and white information film called **‘Better Out Than In’**.

As the film progressed the boys realised the man was stood in one of the classrooms they had seen earlier.

"Now remember farts are funny, they are nothing to be embarrassed about and they should be released whenever the urge arises. The smellier the better I say. Never discourage children from farting and remember our moto Better Out Than In."

"That's certainly not what I heard Professor Bumberclap teaching earlier, and it's certainly not what my parents would say," said Tom holding the flat black disk and wafting it at Ben. "That's far to cool for them."

"Mine neither, I don't understand why Miss Perkins would have that as it's the total opposite of what they teach here?"

Tom thought for a moment before blurting out, "NEVER," and a look of

realisation spread across his face.
"Opposites Ben that's it," as he ran to the opposite walls cabinet and selected the same drawer.

"Look this drawer is labelled "Professor Bumberclap like that one," as he pulled out the matching disk from the 'FOREVER' drawer.

The boys watched in awe as the disk titled 'Farting is not Funny' played with the same man teaching an exact run of the lesson, they had seen the professor delivering earlier that morning.

"You must never encourage them. Remember F-I-N-F farting-is-not-funny."

"OH YES, IT IS," called bat eared Sid from the other room.

"NEVER and FOREVER Ben don't you see? One side is the way they should NEVER teach the parents and other is how they should FOREVER teach them."

Ben gasped, "And Miss Perkins is loading the information into those boxes in the staff room which is then downloading it to the teachers via the cables like a computer would, so that means the teachers are …."

"ROBOTS I KNEW IT," declared Sid running into the room waving his removed sock. "Oh, don't worry our furry friend won't be getting up soon I gave him a little snifter to make sure."

Tom grabbed another drawer and read the label, Madam Clarissa Countenance and another, Miss Prunella Polish, Jaxon Jive, Professor Fredrick Flat the list went on.

Drawer after drawer there was one for each teacher full of floppy black disks all removing the fun of childhood and teaching the parents how to be mean and controlling.

“They have to go, we have to destroy them,” cried Ben pulling open another drawer, “kid kind is depending on us right now, look at all these drawers full of, how did they put it, Sneaky Strategies and Crafty Control. These don’t make Perkins Perfect Parents they make Perkins Pain in the Butt Parents.”

"Nah, swap them," slurped Sid casually on a boiled sweet he had discovered hidden in a tin deep in Miss Perkins desk drawer.

"Swap them?" asked Tom.

"Yeh, swap them so NEVER becomes FOREVER and FOREVER becomes NEVER, simple really," sniffed Sid as he wandered back into the office towards the sweet tin.

"That will take *forever,*" said Ben looking at the lines of drawers, "there are thousands of disks we will be here all night."

"Not the disks silly, the drawers," said Sid returning as he unwrapped another sweet. "Don't worry I've sorted the cat, I put my sock over its nose right at the cheesy toe end he'll be in the land of fairies for a while yet."

Tom and Ben looked at their friend, sometimes just sometimes, there was a flicker of light in the void between his ears that astounded them. That's what made Sid special, but they'd never tell him that.

"Well, what are you waiting for come on I don't want to be here all night."

Sid dragged open a giant drawer and staggered under its weight across the room. One by one they switched the cumbersome disk filled drawers being careful to make sure every floppy disk was neatly in its correct place before moving onto the next. They did not want any evidence they had been there or the switch trick they had deviously pulled.

"Finally that's the last one," yawned Ben as he gave the heavy drawer a push with his aching arms and it slid into its new home.

"Mission accomplished, let's go home I'm exhausted," said Tom as Sid and Ben walked into the headmistress office heading for their ride home.

Tom locked the door and return the key to its sparkly collar home. Sid reclaimed his cheesy sock and they left the snoring Mr Purrkins to his dreams as they braved the heavy scent of oldies and the indescribable pong of teenagers.

"Welcome to Perkins, how may I help you?"

"Oh shut up already," they cried in unison as laughing they jumped in the cleaning cupboard lift and made their escape.

Chapter 12

Yellow Fluffy Teeth

Sid woke with a start. Groggy from a long night and a heavy sleep he picked the bits of straw from his hair and poked snoring Ben and Tom.

Grandpas dry bale filled barn had been the best place to sleep after their eventful night, after all, they were supposed to be at each other's houses.

"Come on Nan will have breakfast on, and I don't know about you but I'm starving."

Removing all evidence of their barn slumber the boys wheeled out their bikes and headed for the farmhouse, the smell of frying bacon and eggs filled the air.

"Morning boys," said Nan as she opened the door and stepped aside. "I was expecting you, so I put extra breakfast on especially for my little gorgeous petal Sidney," as she ruffled Sid's hair.

"Expecting us Nan?" asked Sid straightening his hair worried they had been rumbled.

"The smell of my breakfast always brings you out of that grotty den on a Saturday morning. How you get there so early sometimes amazes me," as she placed three plates of piping hot food before them and several thick slabs of fresh bread and butter.

"Ah-ha well if it isn't my breakfast buddies" announced Grandpa cheerily walking in from his early morning milking run.

Surprised, Nan dropped the bag of mushrooms she was about to add to the frying pan sending them bouncing across the kitchen floor.

"Oh Flo you know why that happened don't you?" asked Grandpa pulling back his chair at the table and joining the boys. "Because there wasn't *mushroom* in the bag."

"Oh Grandpa that's awful," groaned Sid dropping his fork to his plate in mock disgust. A distant chirp signalled the appalling joke's punchline. Poor Steve old habits die hard.

A knowing grin spread across their faces the boys tucked in, enjoying every greasy mouthful whilst Grandpa chatted away and dribbled golden egg yolk down his chin.

"Nan that was amazing, thank you," puffed Sid rubbing his stuffed full tummy and letting out a burp.

"Sidney Welbury that's very rude, excuse me is the word I think you're looking for," corrected Nan waggling her finger at smirking Sid whilst the others tried not to laugh.

Perkins schooling was all around them engrained in every grown-up that had ever been a parent and now they could see it in all its glory.

Little did the grown-ups know things were going to change, they had been rumbled and kid kind would be thanking Tom, Ben and Sid for generations to come. They would be heroes!

Things did not change overnight, no it took time but a few weeks later Tom was rudely awoken when his walkie talkie suddenly crackled into life.

"Are you guys there, you will never believe this," called Sid's excited voice

"What have you done now?" asked Tom with a sigh and yawn. He was not amused at being woken up so early on a weekend.

"Mum just gave me ice cream."

"So what's strange about that apart from the fact it's probably vile banana flavour?" asked Bens sleepy voice.

"For breakfast dim whit," screeched Sid, "she said I could have all I wanted and that healthy breakfasts were out the window. Oh, and get this my dad was in the kitchen singing a song on the radio

with all the right words and everything. He was dancing like a professional on the TV it was amazing."

The miracle was happening, Perkins School for Perfect Parents was slowly creating Kid Perfect Parents.

Tom had to test this out so heading downstairs, trying to be casual he sauntered into the kitchen where Mum was feeding William and his dad was washing up.

"Morning," said Tom trying not to stare at them both and raise any suspicion.

"Morning sleepyhead," replied Mum, "what will it be for breakfast?"

"Chocolate cake with lots of cream, syrup and sprinkles," said Tom matter of fact with not a please in sight. Mum opened her mouth a strange look upon her face before Dad stopped her with a raised hand.

"Coming right up, young man."

Tom tried to hide his delight as the bowl was put before him (no thank you) and he shovelled in the sweet delight. The cream ran down his chin onto his pyjamas and for the finale he picked up the bowl and licked it clean as noisily as he could. Nothing, not one iota of discipline from his parents.

THIS WAS AMAZING!!!!!!!

Tom was bursting to tell the others, so he wiped his filthy mouth with his sleeve and leaving the room with an almighty satisfied burp went to get changed. There was no face or finger waggling, no please and thankyou reminders, no burp correction and certainly no hidden vegetables. They had done it, boy was life going to be good!

Week after week the change in the adults was astounding, they transformed until they became as the three boys has planned.

"What time are you heading home?" asked Sid sat in the deep pile of various crisp and sweet wrappers that were scattered around Den Pippins floor.

"Whenever I feel like it, my mum said I could stay out as long as I want," replied Ben chewing on a particularly sour tasting sweet and showing his yellow fluffy uncleaned teeth.

"Have you got any homework?" asked Tom scratching his unwashed hair and wiping his dirty nose on his even dirtier sleeve.

"Yeah loads but my dad says I can leave it if I want to, apparently it's not that important," sighed Sid.

Sid's grandpa roared from the farmhouse, "SIDNEY WELBURY ARE YOU IN THAT DEN?"

Sid perked up with a smile, someone was checking on him finally.

"Yes Grandpa I'm here, we all are. Do we need to go home?"

"No don't worry lad just checking you were all ok, you stay there as long as you want. Do you want any more sweets or some cake?"

Sid sighed as his shoulders dropped, "NO THANKS GRANDPA WE'RE GOOD."

They could go where they wanted, eat what they wanted and had no rules or discipline whatsoever so why did they all feel so bad?

Tom missed his mums nagging and Dads telling's off. He missed having to be home on time to do his schoolwork and have a bath. He missed Dad dancing in the kitchen and his singing, and he never thought he would say it, but he missed his dads awful jokes. He even missed vegetables……. (I know shocking).

The parks were empty as all their mates were home playing countless hours on games in their rooms and school classes were only half full as pulling a sickie had become so easy the parents didn't mind.

Ben looked at his scruffy lazy friends, it had been fun for a while, but someone had to say it.

"This is boring. I miss my old life."

Sid and Tom nodded, none of them had dared mention it, after all, they created this. It was what they had wanted, so why did it feel so wrong?

“I want my nagging mum back,” groaned Sid.

“There is only one way to put it back, you know, that right?” said Tom looking at his friends. “Are you sure you want to do this because if we put it back that’s it forever?”

Sid and Ben needed no time to think and as they climbed into the cleaning cupboard lift again that evening they were prepared.

"Welcome to Perkins, how may I help you?" called a familiar voice as they ran up the stairs. No map was needed this time, they knew exactly where they were heading.

Thick winter scarves tied over their mouths and noses they navigated the **Teenage Management** floor like professionals. Sid slipped like a ninja into **Bedroom Monstrosity Management** and was out in a flash grappling a wriggling sock in a pair of cooking tongs he'd stolen from his mum.

The sock squirmed and struggled to try and escape as Sid dropped it into the double lined rucksack he had brought for the job.

"Nope still don't want to talk about it," he yelled holding his palm up as they took a deep breath and hurried through the lavender filled **Perkins Perfect Pensioners** department before arrived at back at Miss Perkins office.

An old makeup mirror snaffled from Tom's mum taped to a rusty retractable tractor ariel made the perfect device to check through the glass. The coast was clear apart from a waving ginger tail on the desk chair.

"I got this," said Sid unzipping the rucksack.

The captured sock leapt high from the bag making a bolt for freedom, but Sid was on the ball. Snatching it from mid-air he opened the office door ready to unleash his bomb on poor Mr Purrkins.

With a wail, the large ginger tom flew from his warm master's chair and curled up in his bed quivering in fear.

Sid looked at him with pity, "I don't think he will be a problem this time lads, one sock was enough." He released the desperate red stripy sock and it scuttled away back to its stinky home.

Mr Purrkins did not move a muscle as Tom removed the key from his collar and the boys went about their work. Drawer after drawer they switched each one back and with a wipe to remove any lingering finger marks, they breathed a sigh of relief.

“Let normality return,” puffed Tom as the three walked triumphantly from the room and stood face to face with the illustrious Miss Perkins.

“Good evening boys, I believe you have something of mine,” she said pointing to the key in Tom’s hand. Mr Purrkins was prowling around on the desk a smug ‘now you’re going to get it’ look on his face before he sat down and began to clean himself.

Three hearts beating out of their chests the boys stiffened with utter terror etched across each one’s face. Tom held out the key in his quivering hand and delicately removing it from his palm Miss Perkins returned it to its guardians' collar.

"Please don't kill us," wailed Sid tears forming in his eyes.

"Kill you, oh don't be so drastic silly boy," she squawked with a loud laugh.

Tom looked at the escape door she was blocking, should they make a run for it? No, they would never all make it, they were trapped.

"We know what you have been doing, we know what you are and what happens in this school of yours," Ben said with a quiver in his voice.

"Yes, dear boy I know you do."

"You know that we know?" asked Tom confused as the headmistress walked around her desk and sat down, sitting with a perfectly straight back of course. Mr Purrkins took the opportunity for some attention and climbed onto his mistresses' knee.

"Do you honestly think you could get in here without me knowing? Please give me some credit. I saw you sneaking around watching Nigel in the coffee shop and both times you very kindly visited my school. I believe they call it having eyes in the back of my head. I must say though switching the drawers well that was very clever."

"That was my idea," said Sid proudly which was met with an elbow in the ribs from Ben.

"And you Tom, I see you get your cunning and craftiness from your grandad, he was top of his class in Sweet Snaffling and Evidence Extinguishing. No doubt he would be extremely proud of your exploits."

Mr Purrkins was now living up to his name and purring loudly as his owner's long red fingernails scratched under his chin.

"What are you going to do with us?" asked Tom looking at the now exposed door, "people will miss us you know."

Miss Perkins grinned showing her perfectly straight white teeth. "Nothing at all Tom, you are free to go just like the other children that come to visit me."

“Other children?”

“Yes, do you think you three are the first to discover Perkins School for Perfect Parents? Oh no, there have been others over the years, and all have uncovered the secrets we teach. Each time we’re discovered we change our tactics to conceal our existence but you clever young people are getting smarter every year.”

“Then why are you still here, why didn’t the other kids stop you before?” asked Ben.

“Oh, they tried just like you Ben. You will be proud to know Sidney, one was your grandpa and like you, they soon came to realise we at Perkins are needed in society. Having no order or rules for children isn't as much fun as you thought it would be was it?"

"No Miss Perkins, it wasn't," the three boys admitted hanging their heads.

"I think Perkins has taught you a valuable lesson of your own hasn't it?" she asked looking each Tom, Ben and Sid in the eye. There was a pause for a reply that the ashamed boys never gave.

"Now, I expect no mention of this when you return home, you boys have many years of growing up in front of you. One day it will be your turn to attend Perkins and become a Perfect Parent but for now please close the door on your way out. Oh and Sidney, Nigel says you owe him money for a chocolate cupcake."

Ping! the cleaning cupboard lift signalled its arrival back in the coffee shop. Tom, Ben and Sid watched as the handle turned and the door swung open.

Standing in the light of the closed shop was Nigel the weasel faced man who beckoned them to follow him. Rattling a large bunch of keys he opened the shops front door.

"Nice to see you again Tom, Ben and Sid, safe travels home and remember to keep the secret. We will be watching you."

Standing in the street the boys looked at each other. Nigel locked the door and headed back to his chair for the evening. Not a word had been said since they left Miss Perkins office.

“She knew,” whispered Tom.

“All along,” replied Ben in disbelief.

“Has she really got eyes in the back of her head?” asked Sid as they all walked across the park and headed for home. “He doesn’t look like a Nigel, does he?”

Chapter 13

Guts for Garters

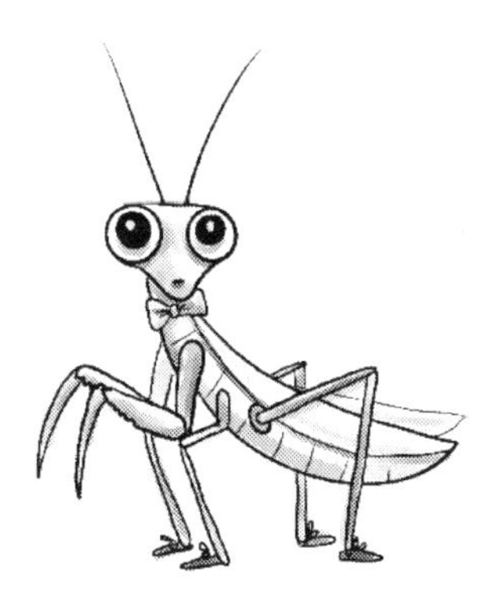

"I think you forgot something young man," said Mum cupping her ear with her hand as she watched Tom digging into his Sunday lunch. "And stop using your fingers you do have a knife a fork you know," as the 'Finger of Doom' danced in disgust.

“Sorry, thank you, Dad,” said Tom with a grin picking up his cutlery.

Things were easing back to normal, well kind of apart from Dad’s dancing that was even worse than normal, apparently, now he had discovered break dancing. Jaxon Jive had a lot to answer for.

“Hey Tom, why can’t a nose be 12 inches long?”

“I have no idea Dad why?”

“Because then it would be a foot.”

“Oh, no dear that’s dreadful,” moaned Mum as baby William threw his bottle of milk across the floor.

Washing up done, Tom grabbed his bike and headed for Den Pippin. The park was bursting with children all getting their daily fresh air and enjoying Bella's ice cream as their mums licked their fingers and wiped their grubby faces.

Ben and Sid were waiting patiently for their friend and as Tom joined them there was a knock on the secret den door.

"Are you boys in there?" it was Sid's grandpa. He pushed the wooden door open carefully and stooped inside the doorway.

"Next time you boys sleep in the barn make sure you close the door properly, anyone could have got in?"

No reply.

"Here I brought you these but don't tell your nan or your parents, they will have my guts for garters," as he handed them each a chocolate bar. Grandpa looked at the boys for a moment waiting for a sign before continuing.

"So you found it then?"

"Found what?" asked Sid with a mouthful of chocolate his cheeks flushing red with lies.

"She's not so mean, a softy really when you know how to play her, but that Mr Purrkins is a vicious thing," as he turned his hand to show a faint claw scar on his palm.

"You should have used a stinky sock bomb," said Sid with a wink.

"That's my boy," praised Grandpa as he closed the door and wandered back towards the farmhouse.

"Ah, Steve nice to see you again, I wondered where you went, we're all missing you. Fancy a cup of tea?"

"You know what's odd though," said Ben. "I'm still getting ice cream and cake for breakfast when I ask for it."

"Yeh, me too," added Tom looking to Sid who was grinning like a Cheshire cat and wiggling his nimble fingers at them.

"Sid's sneaky strategies, well it would be a shame to switch them all back wouldn't it? Now Tom tell us again about this switch idea you keep talking about."

THE END

And in case you were wondering……

* A *dingleberry* is a term for a small piece of poop clinging to the butt of a human or animal. It's sometimes used as a way to call someone "foolish" or "stupid."

The Urban Dictionary

Is your parent a Perkins Perfect Parent?

Bad jokes, awful dancing or just something they do that drives you around the bend.

I would love to hear from you.

dianebanhamimagine@outlook.com
Facebook @DianeBanhamAuthor
Instagram @dianebanham

Watch out for these other titles

I hope you enjoyed Perkins Perfect Parents. If you have a moment to spare, please do leave a review on amazon.

Printed in Poland
by Amazon Fulfillment
Poland Sp. z o.o., Wrocław